MISS HASTINGS EXCELLENT LONDON ADVENTURE

(Brazen Brides, Book 4)

Wealthy banker Adam Birmingham, spurned by mistress, offers marriage to small-town orphan Miss Emma Hastings, who arrives in London to discover her uncle--his neighbor--murdered.

Some of the praise for Cheryl Bolen's writing:

"One of the best authors in the Regency romance field today." – *Huntress Reviews*

"Bolen's writing has a certain elegance that lends itself to the era and creates the perfect atmosphere for her enchanting romances." – *RT Book Reviews*

The Counterfeit Countess (Brazen Brides, Book 1)
Daphne du Maurier award finalist for Best Historical Mystery

"This story is full of romance and suspense. . . No one can resist a novel written by Cheryl Bolen. Her writing talents charm all readers. Highly recommended reading! 5 stars!" – *Huntress Reviews*

"Bolen pens a sparkling tale, and readers will adore her feisty heroine, the arrogant, honorable Warwick and a wonderful cast of supporting characters." – *RT Book Reviews*

His Golden Ring (Brazen Brides, Book 2)
"*Golden Ring*...has got to be the most PERFECT Regency Romance I've read this year." – *Huntress Reviews*

Holt Medallion winner for Best Historical, 2006

Lady By Chance (House of Haverstock, Book 1)
Cheryl Bolen has done it again with another sparkling Regency romance. . .Highly recommended – *Happily Ever After*

The Bride Wore Blue (Brides of Bath, Book 1)
Cheryl Bolen returns to the Regency England she knows so well. . .If you love a steamy Regency with a fast pace, be sure to pick up *The Bride Wore Blue*. – *Happily Ever After*

With His Ring (Brides of Bath, Book 2)
"Cheryl Bolen does it again! There is laughter, and the interaction of the characters pulls you right into the book. I look forward to the next in this series." – *RT Book Reviews*

The Bride's Secret (Brides of Bath, Book 3)
*(*originally titled *A Fallen Woman)*
"What we all want from a love story...Don't miss it!"
– *In Print*

To Take This Lord (Brides of Bath, Book 4)
*(*originally titled *An Improper Proposal)*
"Bolen does a wonderful job building simmering sexual tension between her opinionated, outspoken heroine and deliciously tortured, conflicted hero." – *Booklist of the American Library Association*

My Lord Wicked
Winner, International Digital Award for Best Historical Novel of 2011.

With His Lady's Assistance (Regent Mysteries, Book 1)
"A delightful Regency romance with a clever and personable heroine matched with a humble, but intelligent hero. The mystery is nicely done, the romance is enchanting and the secondary characters are enjoyable." – *RT Book Reviews*

Finalist for International Digital Award for Best Historical Novel of 2011.

A Duke Deceived
"*A Duke Deceived* is a gem. If you're a Georgette Heyer fan, if you enjoy the Regency period, if you like a genuinely sensuous love story, pick up this first novel by Cheryl Bolen."
– *Happily Ever After*

Books by Cheryl Bolen

Regency Romance

Brazen Brides Series
Counterfeit Countess (Book 1)
His Golden Ring (Book 2)
Oh What A (Wedding) Night (Book 3)
Miss Hastings' Excellent London Adventure (Book 4)
Marriage of Inconvenience (Book 5)

House of Haverstock Series
Lady by Chance (Book 1)
Duchess by Mistake (Book2)
Countess by Coincidence (Book 3)
Ex-Spinster by Christmas (Book 4)

The Brides of Bath Series:
The Bride Wore Blue (Book 1)
With His Ring (Book 2)
The Bride's Secret (Book 3)
To Take This Lord (Book 4)
Love in the Library (Book 5)
A Christmas in Bath (Book 6)

The Regent Mysteries Series:
With His Lady's Assistance (Book 1)
A Most Discreet Inquiry (Book 2)
The Theft Before Christmas (Book 3)
An Egyptian Affair (Book 4)

The Earl's Bargain
My Lord Wicked
His Lordship's Vow
A Duke Deceived

Novellas:
Christmas Brides (3 Regency Novellas)

Inspirational Regency Romance
Marriage of Inconvenience

Romantic Suspense
Texas Heroines in Peril Series:
    Protecting Britannia
    Capitol Offense
    A Cry in the Night
    Murder at Veranda House
Falling for Frederick

American Historical Romance
*A Summer to Remember (*3 American Historical Romances)

World War II Romance
It Had to be You

MISS HASTINGS EXCELLENT LONDON ADVENTURE

(Brazen Brides, Book 4)

Cheryl Bolen

Chapter 1

A lady does not enter a tavern. If Aunt Harriett could see her niece now, she would surely perish of apoplexy. For Miss Emma Hastings not only was the sole lady—indeed, the only female—at the tavern at The George Inn, but she had also committed the most deplorable breach of decorum imaginable. She had no chaperon.

Emma should not be chastised for these mortifying transgressions. It was not *her* fault that her uncle had failed to meet the post chaise that had carried her from Upper Barrington to London.

When she'd disembarked from the vehicle and gathered her own portmanteau, she'd been too exhilarated to be alarmed that Uncle Simon was not there to greet her. Such a cacophony of sounds she'd never before heard. Conveyances ranging from pony carts heaped with turnips to grand carriages borne by four matched bays all rattled and pounded along the broad street. The laughter of ragged children, the snarling of hackney drivers, the hawking of flowers from ill-dressed women all fascinated her. Foghorns on the River Thames thrilled the young miss who'd never been farther south than Nottingham. This was a thousand times more exciting than the May Day Fair at Upper Barrington.

She continued to stand beside her portmanteau

in the innyard whilst she waited for Uncle Simon. One hour passed. Had he not received her last letter telling him the time of her arrival? Perhaps he had mixed up the time. Perhaps he had misread her scratchy three for a five. After all, her penmanship was rather lamentable. That had to be it! Uncle Simon would claim her at five.

But five o'clock came and went, and still Uncle Simon had not come. It wasn't as if she would recognize him. She had never actually seen him. Therefore, every man of an age near that of Uncle Simon's five-and-fifty years had drawn her scrutiny. But the lone young woman dressed modestly in sprigged muslin and a hand-knitted red shawl standing beside a large portmanteau drew little scrutiny from any of them.

It was when the rain started to fall that she lugged her belongings behind her and took shelter within the tavern. She'd taken a chair next to a small round table by the window and far away from the taps, hoping none of these strange men would take notice of her. *Never trust a man. All they're interested in is their vile needs.* Or so Aunt Harriett had assured her—not that Emma exactly understood what those vile needs were. Nevertheless, Emma would not risk inciting her aunt's incendiary temper by even so much as making eye contact with any of these men.

She would continue to peer from the window in the hopes of spotting a middle-aged man who might be her uncle.

Though Miss Emma Hastings' knowledge of the world was extremely limited, within a few minutes inside The George, she knew from their voices these men were not from her class. It wasn't that she was nearly as high-and-mighty as Aunt

Harriett, but Auntie *had* raised her to be cognizant of their close kinship to Sir Arthur Lippencott. They must always conduct themselves with propriety—and not be too familiar with sottish men such as those now sharing the chamber with her.

When darkness fell, panic set in. *He's not coming.* There had been some terrible miscommunication. What was she to do? She did not have enough money to pay for a night's lodgings. Or even a hackney ride to Uncle Simon's lodgings at 302 Curzon Street. She hadn't needed money. Uncle was a wealthy man.

With pounding heartbeat, she watched through the frosty window as the lanterns were lighted along the perimeter of the innyard. She knew enough of the world to know that London was its largest city. Thousands and thousands of people resided here. How would she ever find her uncle?

She did know that he lived in the West End and knew his address by memory. Perhaps she could try to walk to his house, though lugging a portmanteau behind her would be difficult.

Drawing in a fortifying breath, she stood and slowly approached the long bar. The man on the other side was talking and laughing with patrons but stopped when he saw her approach. The fellow turned to her, his manner reverent. She was struck over the white hairs threading his bushy black eyebrows. "May I 'elp you, m'am?"

"Indeed you can. Can you tell me if we're in the West End?"

All the men standing up to the bar guffawed.

He did not. He merely shook his head solemnly. "No, m'am. We ain't."

"How long will it take me to walk to the West

End?" she asked.

His eyes widened. "A lady can't go about walking at night."

"You, sir, have not answered my question."

He drew a deep breath. "I suppose a body could walk to the West End in about an hour."

"And which direction would a body walk?" she asked.

He extended his arm forward. "That a way, but we is south of the River Thames. If one wants to go to the proper West End, one crosses the river first, then walks westward that a way. North of the river be a might better place to be walking after dark."

Emma considered leaving her portmanteau in the care of those at the inn, but as it contained all her worldly goods, she could not risk having it stolen. She would haul it herself—even if it would hamper her progress.

As Miss Emma Hastings determined to find Uncle Simon's house, she was equally determined that Aunt Harriett would never learn of her niece's nocturnal foray in the country's wicked Capital.

At least the rain had let up, she assured herself as she left The George. She walked the short distance to the river and stood on the quay for a few minutes, watching the ships and barges float down the busy Thames. All her life she'd wanted to experience this. Fog rose up from the water to obscure from her vision the other side of the waterway.

In spite of the fears which spiraled through her, she was happy to be in London. *I don't want to ever go back to Upper Barrington.* It wasn't that she didn't love Aunt Harriett and wasn't grateful to Auntie for raising her orphaned great niece. But after twenty years living with a stern elderly woman who was considerably older than her friends' grandmothers, Emma was ready for adventure.

She crossed the bridge and was soon in a section of London which was even more bustling than the area she'd just left to the south. This was unlike anything she could have imagined. Even though it was night, all the shops along this busy street were open and brightly lighted. There were so many conveyances on the street, they got snarled, and more than one driver was heard saying words that would have sent Aunt Harriett running for her smelling salts.

It was impossible to walk these streets and not recall Aunt Harriett's tales of women being murdered by the madmen who lived in the Capital. "They've fished their strangled bodies out of the Thames and from the Serpentine in Hyde Park," her aunt had warned.

Emma's heart pounded faster. If she walked very fast, surely no madman would try to get her attention. How, though, did one walk fast when dragging a portmanteau slowed her so wretchedly?

Her arms ached from the bones outward, and she found herself panting for breath that most certainly had dissipated. She had to stop every dozen paces to change hands—and to recover her breathing. Even though she wore gloves, she could tell that the strap had etched into the flesh of her hands.

When the rain returned, she could have wept. Every piece of clothing upon her body got drenched, and with the falling temperatures, she shivered so hard her teeth rattled.

The likelihood of perishing from freezing was far greater than dying at the hands of a madman.

Progress was slow.

She had covered at least a mile, possibly two, when she looked up to see Westminster Abbey. She crossed a street and came to stand in front of the towering Gothic edifice. Here, in front of this awe-inspiring building where kings were crowned and poets were buried, a sense of serenity washed over her. After more than a week of travel—some of it spent with distant cousins to spare the cost of a roadside inn—Miss Emma Hastings felt as if she'd found her home. She stood there for several minutes. Somehow, she knew she'd reached the West End. Her sanctuary.

* * *

Adam Birmingham set down his empty brandy glass and with narrowed eyes observed his brother stride into White's. From the expression on Nick's face, it was clear he was as out of charity with Adam as Adam was with him. The elder brother stormed up to Adam's table and spoke with measured anger. "I thought you must have died."

"A pity a man cannot die of a broken heart," Adam slurred. "I am compelled to keep drawing breath though I've lost the only woman I could ever love."

Nick lowered his long limbs into a chair across from Adam. "I never for a minute thought you'd perished from a broken heart, but I was concerned when you weren't at the bank today. In more than a decade you've never missed a day there. Your staff was so alarmed, they alerted me."

"I drank myself into a stupor last night." Adam shrugged. "Woke up in a strange bed quite late thish afternoon."

Nick eyed the empty brandy glass.

Adam nodded at the waiter, who rushed to replenish it. "Leave the whole bottle."

Nick shook his head. "I'm not staying."

"I wasn't offering. I plan to drink the whole bloody thing. I will drink until I cannot remember the name Maria."

"You're only hurting yourself. It won't bring her back."

"She was the first woman I ever endowed with a house, and look how I was repaid!"

"Has it not occurred to you that there are things other than your wealth that a woman wants?"

Adam scowled. "I should have offered marriage like that Italian bloke who snatched her away from me."

"She obviously wanted marriage, but I'm not saying that you should have offered for her. Were she The One, you would have *wanted* her for your wife. I know it's hard for you to believe now—now when the pain of her loss is so fresh—but you *will* love again. You will find a woman who you will love far more than you ever loved Maria."

"Impossible. Maria was perfection. So beautiful. So talented. So . . . so affectionate."

"Her affectionate nature is likely the reason you didn't offer marriage. She'd been with many men, and you don't want that for your wife."

Adam's black eyes singed. "How dare you impugn the woman I love! Why, if you weren't my duther, I'd challenge you to a bruel."

"You've had too much to drink. Come, let me see you home. Why isn't your driver near?"

"I sent him away. I plan to drink until White's runs out of brandy."

"It's best you drink at Curzon Street. You don't want to humiliate Agar after he sponsored us at White's."

"I'm staying here."

Nick stood. "I cannot persuade you?"

Adam shook his head from side to side with the determined sweep of a contrary lad.

* * *

Many hours later he collected his cape, top hat, and walking stick, left the establishment on St. James Street, and began to walk home.

Then he felt the patter of rain. What a fool he'd been to send home his driver. It was beastly cold—and thoroughly miserable. But even in the state of inebriation he knew himself to be in, he could easily find his way home in a little over five minutes. Better to rush along than to wait in this weather for a hackney.

Not even the thick, silvery fog could disorient him. He'd made the trek too many times. Of course those other times he'd observed the route from the comfort of his luxurious coach whilst his coachman guided them home.

His greatest threat could be footpads. He was, after all, a Birmingham. They were known far and wide as the richest men in the kingdom. Fortunately, there weren't many people out on a wretched night like this.

After he crossed Piccadilly and heard a dragging sound a short distance behind him, the hairs on the back of his neck prickled. He turned around sharply but could see nothing in the soupy fog. Clutching his walking stick which he could use as a weapon, he stood there on the pavement, every sense alert.

There emerged from the fog a girl. Or was it a

young woman? She looked awfully young—possibly old enough to have just left the schoolroom. He would have been powerless to determine the color of her hair for she resembled nothing so much as a wet pup in need of a good meal.

When their eyes met, she smiled. "You look like a gentleman. I have refrained from speaking to any man who was not a gentleman."

So she wasn't a loose woman. Her voice was cultured. He bowed. "Your servant." It was then that he noticed she was lugging a portmanteau behind her. What the bloody hell?

"Could you direct me to Curzon Street?" she asked.

Bosky he might be, but this was a mighty coincidence. Was this some ploy to rob him? He did not respond for a moment. Soft rain slickening his face, he stood there gazing at the young lady. There was something incredibly vulnerable looking about her. She was small of stature and from her dress and lack of sophistication, provincial. As she stood there, shivering, a querying expression on her face, he knew she was sincere. A more innocent face he'd never beheld. "As it happens, that is my direction. I will accompany you there." He eyed her portmanteau. "Please, allow me to assist with your trunk."

She brightened. "Do you know my uncle, Simon Hastings?"

"The name rings a bell, but I daresay it's not someone I know well." If he weren't so inebriated, his recall might be more accurate. He began to haul the cursed portmanteau behind him, wondering what it held but refraining from asking.

The young lady moved to his side. "I shouldn't

like you to think me a doxy or something equally as frightful."

Good lord, he'd never heard that word pass the lips of a gently bred woman. He did not know how to respond. He could hardly tell her that because of his vast experience with doxies he was assured that she was not of their ilk. Instead he merely said, "Anyone would know you are a lady."

"Thank you. Though I have never met my uncle, he's invited me to come live with him in London. I've just arrived today from Upper Barrington, but Uncle failed to meet my coach."

So that explained why the lady was hauling that monstrosity. "Could you not have hired a hackney to carry you to Curzon Street?"

She shrugged. "I have very little money and very little idea of how much a hackney driver would demand for his services."

He stopped and whirled to her, his brows lowered. "This your first-ever time in London? Your first day . . . er, I mean night?"

"Yes."

"Do you not realize how dangerous it is for a young lady to walk about alone at night?"

"Oh yes. My Aunt Harriett has warned me about the madmen in London who prey on women. Since I left the coaching inn. I've raced along as quickly as I could. And I prayed the whole time that the Almighty would keep me safe."

He cast a glance at her. How truly virtuous she must be. "And stupid."

"Pardon? Are you saying I'm stupid?"

He'd thought it, but he hadn't meant to say it. "Forgive me. I'm sure you are not stupid, but it *is* highly unlikely the Almighty will descend into this metropolis to protect a young lady from Upper

Barrister."

Her manner stiffened. "Barrington," she corrected. "Upper Barrington, and you, sir, must be a heathen."

He nodded. "Your Aunt Henrietta would be most appalled over my heathen ways."

"Harriett," she corrected.

He screwed up his (admittedly handsome) face and regarded her thoroughly. "Are you, by chance, a governess?"

"No. I am soon to be learning how to preside over the Ceylon Tea Company, which my uncle owns."

"I say, the fellow who lives next door to me is one of the owners the Ceylon Tea Company."

"Then you, sir, must live next door to my uncle, who resides at 302 Curzon Street."

"Daresay you're right."

They walked along in silence for a good while when he saw the huge lanterns that illuminated Nick's house. He mumbled a curse. "We've gone too bloody far." The fog and the distraction of the girl—not to mention his brandy-impaired state—had caused him to miss turning onto Halfmoon Street.

Ignoring him, she strode to the iron gates and seemed mesmerized by his brother's house. In addition to the abundant lanterns, the courtyard was lighted from rows of huge Palladian windows glowing from abundant candlelight. "I've never seen anything so magnificent! Is this where the Prince Regent lives?"

"No." Though it was said to be the finest house in London. "Me brother lives in that pile of opulentaciousness."

She whirled to him, eyes rounded. "Are you

jesting?"

"About the house or my brother?"

"Both."

"Neither. Would you like to see the house?"

"Oh, I couldn't. Not the way I look at present." She continued to eye him suspiciously. Did she think he was lying about it being his brother's house? Finally, she spoke. "*Opulentaciousness* is not a word. I declare, sir, have you been imbibing strong spirits?"

"I can undersplain. I'm attempting to drown a broken heart."

Her head cocked, she looked up at him and asked, "Did you succeed?"

He shook his head ruefully. "Still remember the vixen's name."

"I see. You meant to drink until you could no longer recall her name?"

"'Twas my intent."

"And what is the vixen's name?"

"Maria."

After a moment of contemplation, she said, "So, do we turn back?"

"Indeed we do."

"So . . . that brother who owns that magnificent house . . . I suppose he's the firstborn."

"He is."

She sighed. "I suppose you wish you were the firstborn to have all the advantages that go with it."

No sense explaining that since they were not nobility, their father had divided his estate equally among his three sons while providing a hefty dowry for his daughter as well as an exceedingly comfortable income for his widow. "The only time I wished to be the eldest was when Nick was bigger than me so I could best him in one of our frequent fights."

"Do you get along now?"

"Brilliantly." *Except tonight.*

They walked in silence for several minutes. She likely believed him a drunkard atheist.

When they reached Curzon Street, she seemed impressed. "These houses are very grand."

"Daresay they're taller than what you see in Upper Barriston."

"Barrington."

He came to stop in front of her uncle's house. It was completely dark, even though the hour was not that late. The houses surrounding it had many lighted windows. "This is your uncle's house. Never been inside of it myself."

Her brows squeezed together. "Does it not seem odd to you that it's the only house without candles? Is this my uncle's custom?"

"No. He's not known to be parsimonious."

"What can have happened to make Uncle fail to meet my coach? To have even stolen away his servants?"

"I'm sure there must be servants—even if your uncle has forgotten you." Not the best choice of words. "Er . . . I didn't precisely mean your uncle has forgotten you."

"I shall find out." She mounted the two steps to the shiny black door and rapped at its equally shiny brass knocker.

A minute passed. She rapped again. Another minute ticked by as she waited.

He let go of the portmanteau's strap. "Here, let me try." He came to stand beside her and rapped at the brass knocker, then pounded upon the thick wooden door with all his strength. His efforts were no more successful then hers.

"Oh, dear, what shall I do?" she asked, her voice more forlorn than it had been in the previous half hour of their acquaintance.0

He froze. A snatch of lucidity sharpened his stupored mind like a magnifying glass to a blurred word. He suddenly remembered why the house was dark, why no uncle had met her coach, why the name Simon Hastings was familiar to him.

The man had died three or four days earlier. Adam's valet had told him all the servants had been forced to find new positions.

But Adam could hardly break such sorrowful news to the girl now. Not after the ordeal she'd endured the past few hours. How terrified she must have been when no one greeted her. Even more horrifying was the prospect of dragging her possessions across the vast and strange city. At night. In near-freezing rain.

He turned to her and smiled. "Not to worry. We'll put you up at my house tonight."

$\mathcal{C}$hapter 2

This gentleman's house might not be as *opulentacious* as his brother's, but it was the grandest house Emma had ever seen. In size, it was no larger than Aunt Harriett's, but where Auntie's house was furnished in dark, ancient Tudor pieces with faded upholstery, every elegant piece of this heavily gilded decor gave a nod to the French. Her eye was drawn to a massive crystal chandelier lighting the entry hall's marble staircase.

A second son he might be, but this man must be exceedingly wealthy—sot or not. She suddenly became shy in his presence.

After greeting his master, the butler quietly locked the massive entry door behind them and took up the long-handled snuffer, no doubt to darken the house now that its owner had returned.

"Tell me, Studewood," the gentleman asked the butler, "which room would be best to put this lady in?"

Studewood's manner did not change one bit as he calmly said, "The yellow room, I should say, Mr. Birmingham. Since the other servants are in their beds, I'll just pop up and see that there's a fire in the young lady's chamber." The butler put down the long-handled snuffer, took the strap to her portmanteau, and started up the stairs.

At last, she now knew this man's name. *Mr. Birmingham.* It seemed a solid name. If he weren't such a reprobate, he'd be . . . awfully appealing. No man in Upper Barrington could match this dark-haired man for handsomeness. Indeed, no man in Upper Barrington dressed so fine, either— not even their revered kinsman, Sir Arthur Lippincott—who actually lived in Lower Barrington. What tailor would not adore clothing a man with such long limbs and trim waist and broad shoulders as Mr. Birmingham? He would show to great advantage any clothing he wore.

"Allow me to escort you to your chambers," Mr. Birmingham said to her.

Their eyes briefly locked. His were dark and piercing. She nodded, then lowered her lashes and began to mount the staircase.

When they were half way up, he paused on a step and swayed as he glanced back at her. "I shappose I should know your name."

Afraid he'd tumble down the stairs, she came to his side. "I'm Miss Emma Hastings. Do give me your arm to hold onto, Mr. Birmingham." She could hardly tell him it was *he* who needed to hold onto her.

"I say, how did you know my name?" He proffered his arm.

"Your butler addressed you."

"Show he did."

They came to the first floor where the entertaining rooms were located and continued to mount the stairs to the next level. Before they rose to the next floor, she tried to take in as much as she could of the tasteful drawing room with its richly patterned carpets, silken draperies, and slender-legged furniture. She was struck that, unlike at Sir Arthur's, the walls of Mr. Birmingham's stairwell were devoid of ancestral portraits. That must mean the Birmingham wealth was new.

One part of her was pleased to be able to stay in this lovely home, even if only for one night, especially since there was no alternative. She knew not a soul in this mammoth city. But another part of her—the part under the influence of Aunt Harriett—kept warning her how dangerous it was to be staying with a strange man. What would she do if he tried to take liberties with her? He was so tall, and she was so small.

Her closest friend back in Upper Barrington, Anne Forester had shared with Emma her six elder brothers' advice on how to thwart unwanted advances. They instructed Anne to kick or to knee the offending man in that unmentionable part of his anatomy. Emma decided she would not hesitate to do that to Mr. Birmingham if he should press those kinds of attentions upon her.

"Let me see," Mr. Birmingham said when they reached the upper floor, "which of these blasted chambers is the yellow?" He stopped and looked down at her. She was still linking her arm to his yet attempting not to show how stunned she was that Mr. Birmingham was not familiar with every room in his own house.

"Studewood did say the yellow room, did he not?" he asked.

She nodded.

His eyes squinted at the door to the second room. "This may be it." He opened the door to a rose-coloured bedchamber, then shook his head.

"Not yellow. Perhaps it's across the corridor." On wobbly legs, he crossed the hallway and opened the door opposite the red chamber. "Ah! Here it 'tis."

Not without trepidation, she swept past him and entered the chamber. She was nearly overwhelmed by its beauty. The bed was swathed in pale yellow silk. A brocade of the same shade covered the walls, and more of the fine yellow silk hung at the chamber's two tall casements. The fireplace, where Studewood was succeeding at starting a fire, was surrounded by a creamy marble chimneypiece adorned with a turquoise porcelain clock. Near the fireplace reposed an elegant chaise of apple green silk, and beside it, her portmanteau. What a home this was! How fortunate was Mr. Birmingham.

Studewood's presence lessened her alarm. Surely, no man would compromise a young woman's virtue in front of his servant. Then she recalled how placidly Studewood had accepted the news that she would be a guest tonight. Was bringing home strange women a customary occurrence for his master? Her heartbeat accelerated as she stealthily glanced at Mr. Birmingham whilst appearing to examine the writing desk, a small gilt table in the French style. He seemed completely disinterested in her.

Thank goodness!

As the coals began to burn, Studewood got to his feet and addressed her. "This should keep you warm all night, miss." With a nod, he left the chamber.

She was about to order her host to leave her sleeping chamber when a curious thing happened. He yawned deeply, eyed her chaise, and collapsed upon it.

For a frightful moment, she thought he had died. Her heartbeat hammering, she raced to the chaise and bent over Mr. Birmingham.

And he started to snore!

She recalled that bosky Jeb Hickman of Upper Barrington had a propensity—after over indulging in spirits, which he most lamentably did with frequency—to fall into exceedingly deep slumber in the most unexpected places. Once in Squire Peterfund's trough, another time in the back of the Widow Pennington's pony cart, and more than once in a pew at St. Stephen's!

What was she to do? She cupped a hand to Mr. Birmingham's arm and shook him. He snored some more. The next time she shook him harder. He snored louder. *Oh, dear.* It was not likely she would be able to rouse him.

She could hardly sleep in the same chamber with a man. Perhaps she could cross the corridor and sleep in the rose chamber. As disappointed as she was to leave this room—especially now that the fire was warming it—she went to the rose room. Though it was even lovelier than the yellow chamber, it felt as if she were standing on a frozen moor. A servant must have left the window open. She strolled across the room and closed the casement. Hugging her own arms, she left the room, knowing she could not sleep there.

From the moment she'd seen her portmanteau in the yellow room, it had seemed like she was meant to be there. The way it claimed her was almost like some kind of Divine proclamation.

Who was there to find out she had (quite innocently) shared a bedchamber with a man? Just so long as Aunt Harriett did not discover the truth. Standing there in front of the fire, Mr. Birmingham snoring in the background, she could almost hear Auntie say, "Once lost, a lady's good reputation can never be regained."

In this, Auntie was likely right. *What manner of man would offer marriage to a sullied lady?* Emma did not want to impede her chances of being some man's wife. She did so long to be married. Before Uncle had invited her to London, Aunt had encouraged Emma to wed. It had been most unselfish of her, too, because Emma knew Aunt Harriett didn't want her to leave.

But Auntie was pragmatic enough to know she was nearing the end of her life. "When I'm gone," her aunt would say, "all that I have will revert back to the estate of my father's lawful heir. You will be alone. And penniless."

For those reasons, Aunt had been pleased when Emma was given the opportunity to make her home in London.

Dare she trust that Mr. Birmingham was truly a gentleman? Could she trust him not to tell anyone he had shared a bedchamber with Miss Emma Hastings? Her gaze fanned to the beautiful bed. How she longed to climb upon it and rest her weary limbs. She was so exhausted, she understood how Mr. Birmingham could have collapsed upon the chaise. She could easily sink down on the mattress and fall into a deep sleep.

Given her lack of alternatives, that is what she would do.

But she could not undress in front of Mr. Birmingham, even if his awakening was about as likely as Uncle Simon knocking upon her chamber door. She tiptoed to her portmanteau and quietly opened it to retrieve her sleeping gown. Then she tiptoed to the bed and climbed upon it. She drew the fully lined bed curtains all the way around the bed for privacy and stripped off the damp traveling clothes she had worn for two days. After slipping into her linen night shift, she buried herself beneath the covers and promptly feel asleep.

* * *

He wasn't at all sure he could lift his head. It felt as if it had been bashed with a cricket bat. Repeatedly. He opened one eye. Then the other. He had fully expected to see the familiar blue bed coverings in his bedchamber, but he did not. Good lord, was he once again waking up in a strange bedchamber? A light rose scent tempered his disorientation. Now that he thought about it, though, he realized he was not actually on a bed. His gaze moved. The first item he spotted was a turquoise clock. He'd bought the blasted thing himself. Did that mean . . . he was at his own house?

He bolted up.

And locked gazes with a young woman who smelled of roses. She was not much more than a foot away from him. She sat in a chair facing the chaise longue he'd slept on. He was about to press some coins into her hands and send her on her way when he thought better of it.

He took a long look at her. The last time he'd seen her, he now remembered, her hair had been wet. Now that it was dry he could tell it was a warm brown, the color of tree bark. Quite an ordinary color. In fact, everything about the young lady was ordinary. She was not a great beauty as Maria had been. Yet all of her features were pleasing. And so was her sweet rose scent.

As for her age, he would put it somewhere

between eighteen and twenty, though she was not much larger than a twelve-year-old girl.

She smiled at him. Her teeth were even and white, and when she smiled, she was pretty—in a quiet way.

Before he could respond, he remembered something else about her. She was *not* a doxy. Even though everything about him was impaired, he knew he had not taken advantage of this girl.

Which made *his* presence in *her* bedchamber all the more offensive. What vile depths had he sunk to? How repulsed she must be over his drunken behavior. How embarrassing that this maiden had likely been exposed to the obnoxious roar of his snores!

He stood and bowed. "Allow me to apologize for my unforgiveable behavior."

She regarded him stiffly, in much the same manner his mother had when he'd been a naughty lad. "It's your home, Mr. Birmingham. Even if you are a Godless hedonist, I am grateful that I had a warm bed in which to sleep, and I shall be even more grateful if you never, ever reveal that you and I shared a bedchamber."

"'Pon my word, I am a gentleman, even if that presently seems inconceivable to you. I'm not always in my cups. I had a very good reason for my intoxication."

"Maria," she said with a nod.

He grimaced. "I told you that?"

She nodded ruefully, then quickly changed the topic. "It was actually awfully kind of you to allow me to stay here. I will own, I was blindsided that no one was at my uncle's house." She stood. "Surely he'll be there this morning. It's no longer raining. I'll just get along. One of Uncle Simon's servants can collect my portmanteau later." She walked toward the chamber door, then turned back. "I beg that you deceive your servants into thinking you slept in your own chamber last night."

At the surfacing memory of who her uncle was, he thwacked his forehead. He needed to tell her the truth. But he'd rather eat his boot than do that. "Don't go."

She raised a fine brown brow and stared at him with her hazel eyes. Perhaps they were a smidgeon above ordinary.

He couldn't stay in a bedchamber with a maiden. "Please, come with me to the library. There's a matter I need to discuss with you."

She followed him from the chamber. As they began to descend the stairs, the clock struck ten. In the ground floor library, he was thankful his servants had built a fire. The mossy green room was toasty warm. He beckoned for her to sit on one of a pair of sofas that faced each other in front of the fire.

Once seated, he was trying to gather the courage to tell her the grim news when she lowered her brows and asked, "Why did you use the word *need*?"

He cleared his throat. "Because I *need* to tell you something before you go bustling over to your uncle's residence."

She gave him a quizzing gaze.

"I'm afraid there's no one at your uncle's house."

"I thought you said you really didn't know my uncle."

"That's true." How in the devil am I going to phrase this?

"When will they return?"

He found himself delaying the response as long as he could. Was that not better—allowing her to ease into the morbid explanation one troubling step at a time? "By *they,* do you mean the servants? Or your uncle? Or both?" He was quite sure he was bungling things most miserably.

"I suppose both."

He drew a deep breath. "Well, the truth of the matter is that none of them are coming back."

"You mean to tell me my uncle has moved?"

"In a way."

"Sir, he's either moved or he hasn't."

She might look young, but there was a distinct maturity about her. He suspected quite a bit of intelligence lurked beneath that youthful exterior. He needed to be direct. He eyed her solemnly and spoke in a voice even more solemn. "Your uncle has died."

Her eyes widened, but not the slightest sound emanated from her. Tears began to trickle along her fair cheeks. After a considerable length of time, she asked, "When?"

He shrugged. "I think three or four days ago."

"And no servants stayed behind?"

"I am told by my servants that they sought employment elsewhere."

"What about my uncle's burial?"

"I honestly don't know, but I am at your service to find answers."

As quickly as the snuff of a flame, she burst into tears. These weren't soft sobs with the intermittent sniffle. This was a full-fledged wail. Every molecule of her body was involved in the convulsion of tears which erupted like a spewing volcano.

He handed her a handkerchief. As he continued to sit across from her, he'd never felt so utterly impotent. She cried and cried. She wailed and wailed. She sobbed as if she'd just witnessed the death of her own child. His handkerchief was completely saturated with her tears. He began to wonder how so small a body could hold so vast an amount of tears. Was there no end?

After an interminable length of time, the clock stuck eleven. Dear lord, had she been wailing for nearly an hour? How long could this go on? Finally, he gathered the courage to ask, "But, Miss Hastings, it is Miss Hastings, is it not?"

Her tear-splattered face lifted, and she nodded.

"I seem to recall that you told me you'd never met your uncle."

She nodded. "That's correct."

Then why in the devil was she so distraught? "Forgive my impudence, but your reaction to his death seems somewhat out of proportion to your connection with him."

She sniffed. "Which makes me seem abominably self centered." Sniff. Sniff. "I'm crying for me. For my future." Wail. Wail. "Or my-y-y-y lack of future." Long wail.

"I would say a young woman like you has a bright future."

She blew her nose and attempted to stop crying. "Since I was my uncle's only living relative, he was going to have me learn about his business. He planned to leave it to me."

"But if you're his heir, it will still come to you."

"Fat lot of good it will do me in Upper Barrington. Because I am an unmarried woman, Aunt Harriett will never allow me to live in London, and . . . " She began to bawl again. "I'd rather die than return to Upper Barrington."

Her aunt must be quite the dragon. "Then you are not of age?" Were she of age, she surely could take her inheritance, hire a companion, and make her own home away from Upper Barrington.

"Not for seven months."

"We shall have to think on your problem, but first we need to discover who your uncle's solicitor is." A helpless little female like her was ill equipped for so urban an undertaking. He would have to help her.

* * *

Perhaps Mr. Birmingham wasn't always such a sot. He *was* being awfully helpful to her. It was quite ingenious of him to dispatch one of his most resourceful servants to Uncle Simon's house to pick the lock.

At first she'd been horrified to be part of such a dishonest activity, but he assured her it was to be considered her house now that Uncle Simon was gone, since she was his only blood relative.

Now she and Mr. Birmingham were in her uncle's library—which wasn't nearly as lovely as Mr. Birmingham's—looking for private papers. She'd been moping around, getting to know a bit about what kind of man Uncle Simon had been by the possessions he'd amassed, the books he'd read.

Unlike Mr. Birmingham's books, which were all classic titles with fine leather bindings, her uncle's were a jumble of assorted subjects and a hodgepodge of bindings, but all looked well read. Unlike Mr. Birmingham's.

Uncle Simon was obviously not a reader of poetry but had a great fondness for travel journals. What a pity he'd repressed his desire to see the world to tend to his business interests in London. Was that why he wanted her to come? Had he planned to have her see to the business while he spent the last years of his life seeing all the places he'd spent a lifetime reading about?

While Mr. Birmingham's home was lovingly looked after, her uncle's was not only cluttered, but it also was not clean. Or perhaps only the library was off-limits to the servants. Had he forbidden his servants to dust and tidy this chamber? It was obvious he spent a great deal of time in this room. The seat of the upholstered chair nearest the fire had been worn to a half-moon shape, and the work table beside it bore circular stains from where glasses had been set.

Her gaze flicked to the other side of the fireplace. That must be where her uncle's guests sat. Indeed, right next to the chair there—a chair that did not appear well used—sat an empty wine glass.

She wondered if the man drinking from that glass might have been the last to see her uncle alive. She shook her head. What an active imagination she had! For all she knew, Uncle Simon had dropped dead at his place of business.

She needed to know more. As his only kin, she needed to know how he'd died and where he'd died. She wanted to know what had killed him.

A pity there were no servants left to answer her questions. If only she had come a few days earlier. If only she'd had the opportunity to meet her uncle.

More than anything, she was curious to know what kind of man he was. How sad that just as their lives were about to intertwine, she was deprived of him. Something inside her ached from the loss.

"Ah, ha!" Mr. Birmingham said after he'd searched through the contents of one of Uncle's desk drawers.

She'd been hesitant to initiate such a search herself. It seemed so disrespectful of the dead. "His solicitor's name is Wycliff. Hugh Wycliff on High Holborn. Hmm. Not far from my solicitor's. Come, Miss Hastings, let us go."

$\mathcal{C}$hapter 3

Once again Miss Emma Hastings was reduced to timidity when she found herself riding with Mr. Birmingham in his lavish carriage. Its luxuriousness was quite beyond anything she had ever seen. The sumptuous seats of pale green velvet were trimmed in a rich gold braid that matched the tassels upon the window curtains. She wondered if the threads were made of real gold. A second son he might be, but Mr. Birmingham was unquestionably rich.

It was rather surprising, really, how kind he was to her—a complete stranger. Would it not have been easier to just offer his coach and dispatch her to High Holborn? It was as if he—an unquestionable sot—empathized with her. How could a man of such privilege so well understand the difficulties facing a lone young woman in a strange city many thousands of times larger than anything she'd ever seen?

Perhaps his kindness was likely to preserve himself from having to endure another session of her tearful hysterics. She must have sounded like gypsy wailer. It mortified her still that she had put on such an exhibition in front of him.

But, truth to tell, she could easily launch into another sobbing fit at the very thought of returning to Upper Barrington.

She wished to express her gratitude to him, but it was as if she'd lost her tongue. She felt so inadequate, like a barnyard hen beside a magnificent peacock. Mr. Birmingham must be accustomed to being with beautiful women who were genteel, well-dressed and clever members of the *haute ton.*

What must he think of her? She peered down at the sprigged muslin dress she'd sewn with her own inferior hand. Aunt Harriett insisted all her day dresses be constructed only of that girlish, modest fabric. Her lack of sophistication would be even more evident by her hand-knitted red shawl. From the glimpses of *haute* fashion she had observed in the pages of *Ackermann's*, she knew the young ladies in London would wear fine merino or velvet pelisses over their morning dresses.

Because of the trajectory of her thoughts, she finally came up with something to say to him. "I suppose Maria was very beautiful."

He was silent for a moment before answering in a woeful voice. "The most beautiful woman I've ever seen. I fell in love with her the first time I saw her upon the stage." Turning to Emma, he added, almost boastfully, "She's an Italian opera singer."

"You met her in Italy?"

He shook his head. "I've never been to Italy. She came to London for an exclusive performance. She'd been the toast of Naples."

Even though Emma had never seen Maria, she would vow that every man in that audience must have half fallen in love with the lovely opera singer. What man wouldn't be honored to win such a woman's affections?

But to Emma's thinking, it was Maria who had

been the lucky one to have won Mr. Birmingham's affections—even if he was frightfully attached to the bottle. He was a very fine looking man. And exceedingly kind. And enormously wealthy. "When did you meet her?"

"Three years ago."

Emma might be a provincial, but she knew enough of the world to know that men did not marry women like Maria. They kept them as mistresses. (Much of Emma's education came from reading the Society columns in the London newspapers to which Aunt Harriett subscribed to.) A man with Mr. Birmingham's wealth would have been able to give the Italian woman anything his fortune could procure.

"She was your mistress?"

He did not meet her gaze but spoke crossly, eyeing his lap. "That is not a topic fit for a young lady's ears."

What had come over her? Emma knew better than to have asked so personal a question. "Forgive my impertinence."

"I daresay you're just unaccustomed to Society."

After they reached the address of Mr. Wycliff's establishment, Mr. Birmingham's coachman opened the door and lowered the step for them.

Mr. Birmingham was kind enough to offer his hand when she disembarked. How interesting it was for her to observe real barristers hurrying along the pavement in long, tightly curled white wigs and flowing black robes.

Every new sight and sound in the Capital exhilarated her. This city's vibrancy never waned, be it day or night. Such a diversity of people and professions she had never thought to see. Upper

Barrington to London was like bread crumbs to a royal feast.

There was so much more she wanted to see. If only she didn't have to return to Upper Barrington. She knew if she went back, she'd never leave. She'd die an old maid just like her aunt. No man there was suited to be her life's mate.

Just as terrifying, once Aunt Harriett died, Emma wouldn't even have a home in Upper Barrington. Therefore, she had been all the more grateful to her uncle for offering to share what he had with her.

Mr. Birmingham proffered his arm, and they entered the three-story building which housed the offices of Mr. Hugh Wycliff.

They located Mr. Wycliff's place of business on the second floor. The solicitor's clerk, a bespectacled man not much older than Emma, looked up from reading one of many dozens of bulging folders which cluttered his desk. "May I help you?"

Mr. Birmingham spoke. "Miss Hastings wishes to see Mr. Wycliff regarding her uncle, the late Mr. Simon Hastings."

The clerk nodded, rose from his desk, and went to an adjoining room. Seconds later he reemerged. "Please, come this way, Miss Hastings. Mr. Wycliff can see you now."

Mr. Wycliff's office was devoid of the piles of papers which cluttered the outer office. His corner office was lighted by eight tall windows and warmed by a red-brick fireplace.

The white-haired, well-fed gentleman stood when she entered, the expression on his face suitably grim, given the sad nature of her visit. "I offer you my most sincere condolences, Miss Hastings."

She nodded solemnly as he beckoned her and Mr. Birmingham to sit in the chairs opposite his desk. Even after he'd muttered his condolences, his face remained solemn and he refused to meet her gaze. Several seconds passed. He gave no indication he would initiate a conversation.

Finally, Mr. Birmingham spoke. "Miss Hastings arrived in London last night at her uncle's invitation, only to learn of Mr. Hastings' death."

"Very unfortunate," said Mr. Wycliff, shaking his head sorrowfully. "Just in the prime of life."

While five-and-fifty sounded quite old to Emma, she realized to a man of the solicitor's advanced years, five and fifty might seem young. "I would like to know when my uncle died."

Mr. Wycliff counted upon his fingers, mumbling under his breath. "Four days ago."

"He's been buried?"

"According to his wishes. He was laid to rest on Tuesday."

"Where?" She was surprised at the moroseness in her own voice.

"In the churchyard of St. Mary Magdalene."

She looked at Mr. Birmingham. "Do you know where that is?"

He nodded solemnly.

Her gaze returned to Mr. Wycliff. "I'd like to know more about my uncle's death. Had he been ill?"

"Not to my knowledge. He was fit and energetic. Seemed younger than his years, and he never missed a day going to his place of business in Southwark."

Her brows lowered. "Then what killed him?"

He shrugged. "We know not. A stomach complaint. His housekeeper said that he must have suddenly turned ill. All the servants had off Sunday, and when she went into the library on Monday morning, she found his body. He'd . . . excuse my indelicacy, Miss Hastings, but there was evidence that he'd . . . cast up his accounts, so to speak."

Tears sprang to her eyes, but this time—to her relief—she spared the present gentlemen her embarrassing display of wailing. The potent earlier tears had been for her own loss of hope. Now they were for her poor uncle. "How sad that he died alone."

Mr. Wycliff inclined his head. "Indeed."

"Miss Hastings would like to take possession of the house on Curzon Street," Mr. Birmingham said. "Do you have the keys?" That he'd been so quick to change the morose conversation convinced her that he feared she'd launch into another crying fit.

Mr. Wycliff nodded. "Your uncle's housekeeper—she's the one who originally came to tell me of his death—gave them to me yesterday after all the servants left."

"Do you know where I could reach her?" Emma asked. She would like to ask Uncle Simon's uppermost servant about him. Her eyes misted again. Now she would never know him.

"Let me see," the solicitor said, opening a drawer of his desk. "I put her direction somewhere. I knew I'd have to contact her regarding her legacy in your uncle's will. Mr. Hastings made provisions for his upper servants." He took out a piece of paper. "Oh, yes. Mrs. Thornton has taken a position at 151 Camden."

He copied it to another piece of paper and handed it to Emma.

Mr. Birmingham stood. "We'll just collect the keys and be on our way."

The solicitor did not respond. He did not make eye contact with either of them, but sat frozen in his chair for a moment. Finally, he eyed Mr. Birmingham. "I'm afraid I can't do that."

"Why?" Mr. Birmingham asked.

"Because the house does not belong to Miss Hastings."

$\mathcal{C}$hapter 4

"What do you mean?" Adam demanded. "Is Miss Hastings not the man's next of kin?"

"Indeed she is. In fact, as far as the deceased was able to determine, Miss Hastings is his *only* living relation."

Adam's intense gaze locked with the solicitor's. "Does the law not state that the next of kin is entitled to the deceased's property?"

"In the event the person dies without a will," Mr. Wycliff clarified.

"Miss Hastings was led to believe—by Simon Hastings himself—that she would come into his property when he died." Adam turned to Miss Hastings. "Is that not so?

Her face stricken, she nodded.

The solicitor cleared his throat. "That happened to be the case. Until last week."

"What occurred last week?" Adam demanded.

"Mr. Simon sent me a new will."

Adam glanced at Miss Hastings, whose brows dipped over widened eyes. He hoped to God she didn't start bawling again. He whipped back to Wycliff and spoke harshly. "He *sent* it to you? Is that not unorthodox? Doesn't a client typically tell you what he wants and have you put it into the proper legal terminology?"

"That's correct. But, as Miss Hastings surely

knows, her uncle is . . . *was* a very busy man. Ceylon Tea was his life, and as co-proprietor of the company, there were always demands on his attention."

"That's why he asked me to come," she said, her voice almost a whimper. "He needed to train to someone take over many of his duties." Her voice hitched. "In fact, he said his half of the business would come to me when . . . " She stopped and drew an unsteady breath. "When he died."

Adam stepped closer to the solicitor, his hands fisted. "Does the business still come to Miss Hastings?"

Mr. Wycliff shook his head morosely.

"I believe Miss Hastings has the right to see this new will."

Her sorrowful gaze went from him to the solicitor.

Wycliff rang a bell, and his clerk entered the chamber. "Be a good lad and fetch Hastings' will."

A moment later, the clerk returned with a large packet and placed it on his employer's desk. Once the door was closed, Wycliff cleared his throat and emptied the contents of the packet onto his desk. He handed Miss Hastings a hand-written document.

Though it wasn't his business, Adam moved to stand over her so he could read her uncle's last will and testament. It started off with the usual language about him being of sound mind, then rather quickly got to the point. "I leave my share of the Ceylon Tea Company to my trusted clerk, James Ashburnham, a capable man who knows the business almost as well as I. It will be left in good hands. In recognition of his faithful service to me, I will to him all my earthly possessions except for legacies to be left to my housekeeper, Mrs. Thornton, and my butler, Boddington, each of whom will receive an annuity of seventy-five pounds for the remainder of their lives. In addition, I bequeath to my niece, Miss Emma Hastings, two hundred pounds annually."

Adam was stunned. Why in the devil would the blighter beg his niece to relocate to London so he could educate her about Ceylon Tea, then while the poor girl was in transit, completely reverse himself? Something was definitely wrong.

Beastly business. The unfortunate Miss Hastings must be in shock. He prayed she wouldn't turn into a watering pot.

"Tell me, Miss Hastings," Adam asked, "have you corresponded with your uncle enough that you would recognize his handwriting?"

She nodded. "I even brought his recent letters with me to London. They're in my portmanteau."

"Does this will appear to be written in his hand?" Adam asked.

"Oh, yes. See the unusual curl on his capital H? That's most distinctive of Uncle Simon's penmanship."

It was an exceedingly neat hand that had penned the document—quite a contrast to the chaos in Hastings' library.

"I'm frightfully afraid, Miss Hastings," the solicitor said, "I have more distressing news for you."

"What more can you take away from this poor girl?" Adam demanded.

Mr. Wycliff eyed Emma. "Are you aware that Harriett Lippincott has died?"

Emma shrieked and clutched at her chest, her eyes widening with shock. "My aunt!"

Adam couldn't blame the poor waif is she launched into another crying fit. Now she really had no blood relation. No home. And she wasn't even old enough to see to the paltry annuity Simon Hastings had settled upon her.

"How do you know about my aunt?" she asked, still not erupting into explosive wails.

His brows furrowed, his voice soft, Wycliff said, "Your aunt's vicar has written to Mr. Hastings, informing him that he was now to stand as guardian to you. All of your uncle's mail now comes to me."

Adam turned to her. "Do you have any more blood relatives?"

She shook her head and began to softly weep.

Adam addressed the solicitor. "Will Miss Hastings need a guardian?"

"How old is she?"

"She doesn't reach her majority for seven months."

Wycliff winced. "The Court of Chancery will have to appoint one for her."

"Please start the proceedings," Adam instructed. He suddenly felt compelled to remove Miss Hastings from this scene of harrowing news. He squeezed her shoulder. "We'd best leave now, Miss Hastings. After the sadness which has greeted you your first day in London, you must do something fun, and I'm putting myself at your service."

Tears trickling from her eyes, she offered a wan smile and rose, nodding to Wycliff as she left the chamber.

When they reached his coach, he tried to ignore her state of grief. Holy, bloody hell. Either of those pieces of bad news would have been enough to crush a strapping man. Was there not something he could do to divert her thoughts from such devastation? "Pray, Miss Hastings, you must tell me what you would most like to see in the Capital. Should you like to climb atop St. Paul's? Or take a stroll through Vauxhall Gardens? Perhaps see Poets Corner at Westminster Abbey or look at the exhibits at the British Museum?"

She made no response. She merely looked straight ahead with unseeing eyes. To his consternation, those bluish green eyes of hers started to mist again. *Oh, no.* He instructed the coachman to drive through Hyde Park. Surely all the finery that was sure to be on display there would fascinate a girl from a small village.

But as soon as the carriage door was closed, her tears came. Great, gushing tears accompanied by heaves and woeful whimpers. She cried all the way from The City to Westminster. She bawled from Westminster to Mayfair. When they entered Hyde Park he tried to divert her attention. "I say, Miss Hastings, I do believe you'll enjoy seeing the fashionable people in Hyde Park."

She didn't even lift her curtain.

He handed her a handkerchief. Good Lord. She was like a living, breathing spigot! He wondered if this was to be The Cry That Never Ended.

Rotten luck. His.

Why in the devil can't I be one of those men who can turn a cold shoulder to a suffering woman? But, no, he would do anything in his power to ease her pain. The pity of it was, there did not seem to be a thing he could do to take her away from her grief.

Rotten luck. Hers.

Was there not something he could do to lift her

thoughts away from this shabby business?

He almost wished Simon Hastings was still alive so he could bash in his face. Such thoughts were of no help to the sobbing wretch beside him. He must concentrate on what he could do to eradicate her cries and bring a smile to her youthful face. He remembered the look of child-like pleasure on her face when she'd glimpsed Nick's *opulentacious* house the previous night. And Nick's house was only minutes away from Hyde Park.

He tapped on the roof of his carriage with his walking stick and ordered his coachman to take them to his brother's house on Piccadilly.

Though the situation, in his mind, demanded that he speak to the sobbing creature in a gentle voice, he forced himself to use a commanding voice. "Miss Hastings, you will have to pull yourself together. I must go to my brother's, to that house you so admired last night, and we can't have you bawling like a baby." He hated himself for being so reproachful to a lady in distress, but kindness had not succeeded.

This approach seemed to work. She took a deep sniff, dabbed at her eyes with the handkerchief, and finally spoke. "Forgive me."

Something in her forlorn voice went straight to his heart, melting it as heat to butter. He moved across the carriage to sit next to her, to gently cup her shoulder reassuringly.

Now his voice gentled. "There's nothing to forgive. You have every right to show your unfathomable grief. Either one of the sad intelligences you've been dealt today would make a grown man bawl. You may very well wish to cry a river, but it will not help. I know you have always wanted to see London, and I won't allow you to return to Upper Bannington until I personally show you the sights of London."

She sniffed. "Barrington. Upper Barrington." Then an anguished sob broke from her, and once more, she was overcome with a crying fit. "The pity of it is I never wanted to return there—and now I cannot. My aunt's property goes to her father's heir."

He curled his arm about her slender, heaving shoulders and was once more aware of her light rose scent. How wretched the poor girl must be. He'd never felt more impotent. He'd always been a problem-solver. And a successful one, to be sure. But when it came to women, he was clueless.

Did they not like hats? "My dear Miss Hastings, before we go to my brother's I should like to take you to London's finest milliner and have you select a new hat." Surely that would cheer her. Maria had certainly loved getting new hats.

She buried her face in her hands and cried harder. "It saddens me that Auntie died alone and that I never said a proper good-bye. That I—the only person who loved her—wasn't there at the end."

"I believe she knew the end was coming and she wanted to spare you. She wanted you to be happy in London."

She brightened. "I believe, Mr. Birmingham, you are right."

He patted her. "Please, Miss Hastings, do quit crying."

Miraculously, her tears cut off as if they had been snuffed. It was a moment before she lifted her tear-stained face to him. Her (perfectly formed, actually) nose was red, as were the whites of her eyes, and he thought he'd never seen a more melancholy face.

He was reminded of his mother's ingrained belief that one could die of a broken heart. He'd never believed such rot, but he did worry that this poor lass's grief was so profound she could perish from it. Simon Hastings' blasted will had crushed her as surely as a boot stomping a shard of glass. Then she lost the closest thing she'd ever had to a mother. Both in the same day.

She seemed such a fragile little thing. Even if she would reach her majority within the year, it was difficult to believe she would be one-and-twenty.

"Thank you most sincerely for all you kindnesses to me, Mr. Birmingham." Her voice had started to break on his name. She stopped, then continued in a more firm tone. "I feel wretchedly guilty that I've been such a burden to you, that you've had to see my crazed weeping."

His arm still hooked around her, he patted her shoulder. "You're not a burden."

"Oh, but I am! You've spent your entire day on me." She drew a breath. "I did so appreciate you going with me to Mr. Wy-y-y-y-" She never got Wycliff out before another cry broke. But she quickly gathered her composure and continued. "Mr. Wycliff's office and acting on my behalf."

"I was happy to do so."

"I never realized heathens could be so nice."

He chuckled. A provincial like her would think him debauched. He only hoped his mother didn't come to think him a heathen.

"If I weren't here, what would you be doing with your day?"

"I'd be at my bank. Yesterday was the first time

I've ever missed going since I took over the bank when my father died."

"How old were you?"

"Same as you are now." Thank God she was getting her mind off her troubles. "Ten years ago."

"Then I feel doubly guilty for stealing you away."

He placed his knuckles beneath her chin and eased her face closer to his. "Do you not think I've earned a day of fun?"

She burst out laughing. "This cannot have been fun!"

"Ah, but it will be when I show you my city."

The coach had stopped at Nick's, but he'd sent the coachman back to the box. He removed his arm from her. He had gotten far too intimate. He must show Miss Hastings he was a gentleman.

"I should like that," she managed in a whimpering voice. "I have always wanted to be in London." She began to cry again, all the while trying to articulate, "Where will I live?"

Where *would* she live?

Her melancholy was like a hammer to his already broken heart. He hated to see her pain. He'd been in pain when Maria left. Still was. At this moment, making Miss Emma Hastings happy was the most important thing in his life.

And he had the means to do so.

"I know how you can stay here."

"What could you possibly think of to allow me to stay in London?"

"I propose to make you my wife."

$\mathcal{C}$hapter 5

Good Lord! What had come over him? For more than a decade he'd skillfully evaded scheming fortune hunters. Beautiful debutantes, aristocratic ladies from ancient families, and a never-ending stream of opera dancers had all tried to snare him—and his enormous fortune—since the day he reached his majority nine years previously.

His firm resolve not to wed had now been shattered by one bawling female.

Her eyes widened, and her mouth opened into a perfect oval. That melancholy countenance which had captured his sympathy was replaced with one of utter shock. "I cannot have heard you correctly, Mr. Birmingham. Surely you did not just offer for a woman you met only last night?"

He shrugged as casually as one who'd just suggested a spring-day stroll. "I did. If you knew me better, Miss Hastings, you would know that Adam Birmingham never deceives. When I ask for something, I go through with it." He managed a grin. "And I always get what I want."

Her eyes met his. Hers looked almost gray in the carriage's dim light. And they were intense. "Except for Maria," she murmured.

Maria's name was like a swift kick to his gut. If there had been any hope of rekindling his *affaire de coeur* with Maria, he would never have asked for Miss Hastings' hand. But Maria was now happily married to her count and returning to the country of her birth. He frowned. "Except for Maria."

"How can you offer for one woman when your heart belongs to another?"

He could not deny that he was still in love with his former mistress. "If I can't have Maria, I want no other. I'll not love again. I'll never marry. Why not solve your problem instead? That would lessen my melancholy."

"As much as your proposition would solve my problem, I cannot allow you to throw yourself away on an unsophisticated woman of modest means."

"But Miss Hastings, the means of my wife matter little. I'm an extremely wealthy man."

"Look at me, sir. I must be a far cry from the beautiful, fashionable women you are accustomed to."

She spoke the truth. He had always associated with beautiful women, women far lovelier than she. They had all been fashionable, too. As his gaze locked with hers, he realized that while she was not a stunning beauty, she was subtly pretty. With fashionable clothing and accessories, she might become something quite above the ordinary. "As my wife, you would possess the most beautiful clothing, jewels, and furs in the kingdom."

Her eyes widened. She swallowed hard. "You make it very difficult to refuse."

"Good. Shall we set the date?"

"But I do refuse."

He did not respond for a moment. "You wound

me, Miss Hastings. Spurned by two women in the same week. I shall have to do myself in."

"You're making this very difficult, Mr. Birmingham. Your offer is the most exciting thing that's ever happened to me." She blew an impatient breath. "You've been so kind. I would never hurt you."

"Then you ought to marry me."

"One does not repay a rescuer's kindness by destroying one's rescuer."

"You think marrying you would ruin my happiness?"

She nodded. "You can't realize it now. Now you are too hurt by Maria's rejection. But pain lessens over time, and when it does you will want to love again. You'll want a wife worthy of you, and I'm not that wife."

"I beg that you not put me on some pedestal. I would wager I come from far more humble origins than you. Tell me, Miss Hastings, is there any member of your extended family who bears some kind of title?"

She bit her lip. "My mother's great uncle is Sir Arthur Lippincott, a baronet."

"There you have it! Your family's more illustrious than mine."

"I still refuse to make your life miserable."

Why in the devil was he pleading with this woman to marry him? He'd never wanted marriage. Or, as Nick had told him at White's last night, he didn't want to marry until he met The One, and Emma Hastings was most certainly *not* The One. This woman was giving him the chance to bow out gracefully and preserve his cherished bachelorhood. Yet he kept begging her to marry him.

Had he taken leave of his senses? Since Maria had run off with Count Cuomo, he had been convinced he would never know happiness again. Why not bring some happiness into this lady's life? Even the small services he'd been able to perform for her today had made him happy. He would seek his happiness by helping to fulfill this young woman's dreams.

"It would give me great pleasure to be the author of your awakening womanhood, to introduce you to the world's greatest city, to have some small part in your transformation from pretty young thing from Upper Biddington to London's most fashionable matron."

"Barrington. Upper Barrington," she said with a mock indignation that was belied by her furtive smile.

Ah, a smile! He'd managed to pull her from the doldrums! Perhaps his job was done. No need to keep hounding her to wed him.

Her voice sounded youthful when she wistfully said, "I had always hoped to marry for love."

So had he.

"But, my dear Mr. Birmingham, had I to choose between forfeiting love or forfeiting London, I choose to forfeit love."

Had she just accepted his offer of marriage? His stomach plummeted. Oh, God, what did he do now?

He took her hands in his and spoke huskily. "I hope to make you very happy, my dear."

"Please," she whispered hoarsely, "call me Emma."

"And you must call me Adam."

"It's not to be a real marriage, is it?"

"Of course. I will procure a special license and

marry you at the earliest convenience. I will make all the proper financial settlement on you."

"That's not what I meant by a *real* marriage."

He suddenly understood. Unaccountably, his gaze flicked to her modest bosom. She was a woman, after all. And he was a man. He should have anticipated her query. "Quite right."

"What do you mean by *quite right*? Will you or will you not take your conjugal rights?"

How in the blazes did a girl from Upper Something or Other know the meaning of the word *conjugal*?

"I should think that one day you'll want children," she said.

Oh, God. He'd forgotten about that. He did want children one day. But he did not want to force himself on this poor maiden. "I shall conduct myself as a gentleman. The discussion of children can be dealt with at a time in the distant future."

As unsettled as he was, he needed to be pragmatic. He must discount that gloom which hung over him because he was entering a loveless marriage. He must back up his well-meaning proposal with a plan of action. The girl needed a strong, commanding man in her life right now, and that is exactly what he meant to be.

Despite his creeping misgivings.

"Well, then, my dear M-m-, er, Emma, I will need to procure a special license—and I shall need to install you in respectable lodgings until I have the honor of claiming you for my wife. You will, of course, stay here at my brother's *opulentacious* house. I think you will be happy with his wife. But before you do, I believe you would prefer looking a bit smarter."

* * *

Nothing was to be done today about her modest dress, but dear Mr. Birmingham spared no expense in purchasing for her a half a dozen new bonnets—one of which perfectly complemented her sprigged muslin, making her dress appear far lovelier than it actually was. He also bought her a new Kashmir shawl the colour of freshly churned cream, and he took her to what he said was London's finest modiste.

At Madame De Guerney's establishment on Oxford Street, Emma almost forgot her shabbiness for Madame De Guerney herself treated her as if she were a royal princess. "Ah, but mademoiselle's delicate appearance will do great credit to my creations," she'd said as she took Emma's measurement.

Emma actually felt like a royal princess as Mr. Birmingham insisted she select patterns and fabrics for a half a dozen morning dresses as well as a half a dozen ball gowns. When Madame De Guerney showed her the vast array of fabrics, Emma's eyes widened. She felt as if she were in a dream. She'd never thought to see so many beautiful fabrics all at once. Fine silks rustled. Whisper-thin muslins were as soft as goose down. There were everyday bombazines and high-quality linen for shifts. Sumptuous velvets ranged in colour from deep crimson to powder blue. Emma thought she could have spent an entire day ogling at Madame De Guerney's. She'd never imagined such a place existed.

Madame assured Mr. Birmingham all the dresses would be delivered to Curzon Street within five days. Emma was shocked that twelve dresses could be constructed in so short a time, but the modiste explained that she employed a large staff of needlewomen to fulfill her client's orders. "And if I had to stay up around the clock myself to ensure delivery, I would. Mr. Birmingham's satisfaction is paramount to me," Madame De Guerney said.

Emma wondered if this was where Maria had come to have her dresses made. She glanced at Mr. Birmingham, and her heartbeat accelerated. How very handsome he was. How excited she was to become his wife—even if she wasn't a *real* wife.

But most of all, she thought of how jealous she was of Maria.

What a pity he still loved his former mistress. What a pity that Maria's betrayal had spoiled him for all other women.

After they left the dressmaker's, Mr. Birmingham insisted they go to Rundell & Bridge. She had seen their adverts in the London papers and knew this was the jeweler to royalty. Her heartbeat soared.

Inside, Mr. Birmingham asked her to select a ring that would symbolize their marriage. The eager jeweler—who obviously knew Mr. Birmingham well—showed her a square ruby wreathed in diamonds, along with a band constructed of identical emeralds as well as a plain band of gold.

She hoped she would not displease Mr. Birmingham, but she selected the simple gold band.

"You're not doing so because it's less expensive?" he asked. "I assure you, I can afford anything you should desire."

She shook her head. "Because of my small stature, I prefer simple pieces. I hope you don't mind."

He smiled down at her. "It's your hand it will go on. Once we've wed, of course."

Her heartbeat roared. *I can't believe I'm going to marry this man.* In her wildest dreams, she had never imagined she would marry a man who embodied so many sought-after traits. With such handsomeness, wealth, and, most especially, kindness, she could overlook his sottishness. Though she would have to do everything in her power to get the man to church!

After they selected the ring, he decided to make a few selections of his own. "My wife will need jewels."

Silken trays of spectacular necklaces were unveiled. Many-tiered diamond necklaces vied with a ruby pendant and another necklace of scalloped emeralds. All of these were accompanied by matching bracelets.

"Oh, no," she protested. "These are far too grand for me."

Mr. Birmingham scowled down at her. "Remember, Emma, you are to be the wife of one of the richest men in England. You are to dress appropriately."

She felt as if she'd just been scolded. "I assure you, M- - -." She stopped herself. She mustn't address him so stiffly in front of Mr. Bridge. After all, he was to be her husband. "Adam, I have no experience with fine jewels. I beg that you make the selections for me."

His brows lowered. "Are you sure? I wish you'd exert your opinions."

"I have no opinions when it comes to fine jewelry."

Their eyes held for a moment. She thought he was going to protest, then his gaze softened. It was as if he understood she was afraid of humiliating herself. "Very well, my love, I will select your jewels."

She could have fainted. He'd called her *my love*! She knew he was merely doing so for the benefit of the jeweler. Mr. Birmingham wouldn't like it broadly known that he was marrying a country miss who was practically a stranger. Still, his endearment made her feel as if her heart were expanding out of her chest.

Mr. Birmingham walked along the showcase and came to pause. He eyed a pearl and diamond choker. "I should like to see how this looks on my betrothed."

"Please," Mr. Bridge said, "feel free to try any of these on your lovely lady."

Lovely lady. No one had ever referred to her as a lovely lady before, but she was actually beginning to feel lovely, to feel as if she'd been transformed by some wizard's wand.

Adam took the necklace and came to place it about her slender neck. The brush of his hand as he clasped it gave her another of those chest-expanding experiences. Her breath grew short. No man had ever touched her before.

She had been astonished over his selection for it was the one in all the store that she thought most compatible with her plain appearance.

After he clasped it, he stood back and peered at her. Her breath hitched when she realized his eye skimmed her breasts—not that there was much to differentiate her from a lad. But she did possess a modest bosom, and for the first time in her life, she actually fancied the idea of a man being interested in her feminine jigglies.

His face lifted with pleasure. "Perfection. It's

simple and elegant, just like my dear Emma."

What talents Mr. Birmingham possessed! He could rival Edmund Kean on the stage.

"Of course, my dearest, you will need one necklace that must be exquisite, that will proclaim you to be the grandest lady in all of London."

"But . . . dearest, I am *not* the grandest lady in London."

He merely gave her a smug smile. "Oh, but you will be."

"I have just the necklace!" Mr. Bridge went to the back room and returned with a large velvet box. "While we normally create our own jewelry at Rundell & Bridge, this is a very special commission we were able to obtain from a member of the Bourbon Royal Family."

Emma's pulse rocketed. Could this actually be happening to her? Emma Hastings, an orphan from Upper Barrington?

As the top lifted from the purple box, Emma gasped. She had never seen anything so lovely. The necklace's focal point was a net of diamonds which held a small but skillful "bouquet" of amethysts. Of course, it was much too grand for her.

"Allow me," Adam said as he took it and draped it around Emma. She peered at herself in the looking glass and swallowed. Even if it was far too *opulentacious* for her, she loved it.

Adam nodded his approval. "Yes, Mr. Bridge, this will do very nicely." Turning to Emma, he added, "I believe we will have to send a note around to Madame De Guerney to change the green gown to some shade of purple to wear with this. Do you agree, my dearest?"

This necklace with a lavender gown would be,

to use Mr. Birmingham's own word, *perfection.* She nodded shyly. She felt like an interloper. What had she ever done to deserve to be treated like a princess?

She could never repay Mr. Birmingham for his many kindnesses, but she vowed she would find a way. Even if it took the rest of her life.

When he came to remove it, he said, "It's very lovely on you."

"Are you sure you can afford it?" she whispered. "He didn't mention a price."

He laughed. "Yes, my darling bride-to-be."

She felt like a great hoarder after all the beautiful things that had been bestowed upon her that day.

As they rode back to his brother's palatial house, Emma reflected on her stupendous good fortune. In the span of a single day she had gone from the depths of despair to an elation unlike anything she had ever thought attainable.

Though still stunned by the news of Aunt Harriett's passing, Emma took comfort in Mr. Birmingham's explanation. Auntie was close to ninety. She must have been waiting until she thought Emma was being taken care of. She wouldn't have wanted Emma to be melancholy.

Thanks to Mr. Birmingham, her grief was being assuaged.

I am going to be married to the finest man in the kingdom. She was so exhilarated, she felt as if she'd just downed an entire bottle of champagne. (She only hoped her intended avoided champagne—and all other spirits. She wouldn't like him to turn into a Jeb Hickman.)

When the coach entered the courtyard at his brother's house, all the lanterns glowed now that night had fallen. Once more, she became cognizant of how shabby she must appear to a couple who lived in so fine a home. They must be the toast of London. Even if the Birminghams were not possessed of pedigree.

He turned and took her hand. "You will love Lady Fiona. She's one of the warmest people I've ever known."

Lady? Had he not said his family lacked pedigree? Now she was more nervous than ever.

$\mathcal{C}$hapter 6

She spun around to face her intended. "I thought you said there were no aristocrats in your family!"

"Lady Fiona's not a blood relative."

"Your brother married a member of the nobility?"

Adam shrugged. "All things are possible when one's pockets are deep. Not that I care a fig about titles. And I assure you none of my siblings who've married into the nobility did so purposely. They all married for . . . " He paused. Swallowed. "For love."

His comment pricked her exuberance. He would be deprived of a loving marriage because of her. She drew a breath, then recalled his words and was stunned. "How many of your siblings have married into the nobility?"

The coachman opened the door. She shook her head. "Please, Adam, not yet. I can't go in there just now."

He nodded sympathetically and spoke to his servant. "Give us a moment."

She felt only slightly more at ease when the coach door closed and it was just she and Adam sitting in the dark carriage.

"Actually, all of my siblings, but I assure you two of the three fell in love without knowing their loved ones came from noble families."

"How can that possibly be?"

"My sister and the Earl of Agar—Lady Fiona's brother—admired each other from afar for many months of morning rides in Hyde Park. And the story of my youngest brother's courtship with Lady Sophia is quite an amusing one. She pretended to be someone else when she first met William, and even when he thought she was what he has referred to as a Shady Lady, he fell quite desperately in love with her."

"What about this brother who lives here?"

"That's another amusing story. Lady Fiona—who is quite beautiful—actually asked Nick to marry her. She needed his fortune to save her brother from Spanish bandits."

"Then neither of them loved when they married?"

"Supposedly not."

"Do you believe Nick married her for her family connections—and her beauty?"

Adam puckered his lips. "I believe he loved her from the moment she came to him, but he would not admit it. "

"And it's been a successful marriage?"

"They are besotted over one another. I will own, it took some time before either would express their true feelings."

For a fraction of a second she allowed herself to hope that a marriage between Adam and her would grow into a powerful love. Then, she sank into melancholy. She needed to release Adam. If she weren't standing in the way, he could also marry one from a noble family. He could marry a beauty like Lady Fiona. He could marry for love.

She had no right to deprive him of happiness. "I

can't go in there. I don't belong. You deserve someone like Lady Fiona."

He took her hand and spoke gently. "I told you. Titles don't matter to me. And you, my dear Emma, underestimate yourself. With all your new finery, you will be one of the loveliest ladies in all of London. Did you not hear how Madame De Guerney praised your elegance? I assure you, that woman has a reputation for being ruthlessly blunt. If she thinks you're pretty, the *ton* will think you pretty." He squeezed her hand. "I think you're pretty."

That one little compliment that likely meant nothing to him buoyed her and actually made her feel as if she *were* pretty. She did so want to marry him. "Lady Fiona is sure to think me a country mouse."

"Lady Fiona's not like that. You will see. When she first married Nick and found out he had a natural child ensconced with caretakers, she insisted the little girl come to live with them. She has raised that little girl as if she were her own daughter. And, mind you, the child's mother was not fit to be in the same house as a sweet little girl."

"Then I will be very happy to make Lady Fiona's acquaintance."

* * *

"Surely the Prince Regent's house cannot be as grand as this," Emma exclaimed when she found herself in the soaring, candlelit entry hall of Nicholas Birmingham's mansion.

Adam shrugged. "I've never been to Carlton House, so I cannot judge. Ask my brother. He and Lady Fiona have been there."

"Did your brother build this house after they

married?"

He shook his head. "No. My brother commissioned it before he ever knew Lady Fiona."

"He's certainly possessed of exquisite taste."

Adam looked up the broad, gilt-railed marble staircase as his brother and his wife came down, calling out a greeting.

When she looked up, Emma was astonished. Nicholas Birmingham looked so much like Adam, they could almost be twins. Of course, she found Adam the more handsome. She also easily understood why it would have been no sacrifice for Lady Fiona to have offered herself to Nick.

Emma looked back to her betrothed. "Does the third brother also resemble you and Nick so strongly?"

He chuckled. "Not at all. He's neither tall nor dark, but he's quite the most handsome of the three."

She doubted that.

If she'd been dazzled over this house, she was speechless over Lady Fiona' loveliness. Nick's wife was of average height—which was two or three inches taller than Emma. Her figure was perfection, slender where it should be and rounded in the appropriate places. Her pale blonde hair feathered with flawless ivory complexion contributed to an icy elegance.

But it was her beautiful face that captured Emma's full attention. Emma could no more have refused to smile back at Lady Fiona's charming countenance than she could destroy a painted masterpiece.

"Lady Fiona," Adam said, "I should like to present to you the woman to whom I am betrothed, Miss Emma Hastings."

How the lady managed to retain her sweet smile while shock registered on her face baffled Emma. And made Emma greatly admire her.

Lady Fiona need not say a word because her husband made the appropriate—or perhaps, in his case, given his sharp tongue, *inappropriate*—responses. "What the devil? You cannot be serious."

Anger flittered across Adam's face, but he managed to control it. "Pray, my dear brother, have a care for Emma's feelings. I most sincerely do desire to make this woman my wife."

Lady Fiona stepped forward. "Welcome to the family, Miss Hastings."

"Please, call me Emma."

Nick then gathered his composure and bowed at Emma. "Forgive me if I have made you uncomfortable. I meant no offense."

She bestowed a smile upon him. "None taken. The betrothal came rather suddenly. It's only natural you'd be shocked."

Still smiling, Fiona addressed her. "Should you like a tour of our house? I am told it is one of the attractions of London." She directed a worshipful gaze upon her husband. "All owing to my husband's talent for design."

Now Emma gazed admiringly at him. "You served as your own architect?"

He shrugged.

As handsome as he was, she was now certain he was not as handsome as Adam.

"I did hire an architect to implement my ideas," he said.

"But Nick was the one who insisted on bringing in an Italian artist to paint the ceilings, and almost everything here that visitors admire was envisioned by my husband."

"No more praise, please, love," Nick said, his voice stern.

Lady Fiona slipped her arm through Emma's, and they began to stroll about the *opulentacious* house while Adam and his brother went to the library.

* * *

He had dreaded breaking the news of his nuptials to Nick. Just the previous night Adam had been subjected to a lecture from him, and now Nick was sure to launch into another about marrying a woman he'd only just met. He fully expected Nick to encourage him to wait for The One.

Once in the library with the door closed, Nick calmly poured each of them a glass of Madeira and instructed Adam to take a seat on the sofa which faced the fire. Nick turned a wooden chair away from the fire to face the sofa, then he launched into his elder-brother admonitions. "You can't be serious about marrying that young woman."

"I know it's sudden, but I am resolved."

"Do you not still fancy yourself in love with Maria?"

"Of course. I will love Maria until I draw my dying breath."

Nick rolled his eyes. "I will own, I was shocked when you made your announcement. I regret any embarrassment or hurt feelings I may have caused Miss Hastings. She seems to be a nice young lady. And quite the opposite of any woman who's ever appealed to you."

"That's true."

"Then why in the devil did you offer for her?

And less than four-and-twenty hours after getting yourself senseless with drink for the love of your opera singer."

"It's precisely because I shall never love again that I have offered to brighten Miss Hastings' existence. I take my consolation in that."

"What the bloody hell does that mean?"

Adam proceeded to tell his brother about his meeting with Emma the previous night, about her sleeping at his house, and lastly about the onslaught of sad news she'd learned at the solicitor's that morning. He and Nick had always been completely truthful with one another, and this was no exception.

The fire outlining his head and shoulders like some Renaissance masterpiece, Nick listened intently, nodding occasionally as Adam spoke.

When he finished, Nick nodded and said, "Of course you had to offer for her after sharing a bedchamber with the young lady. You know how servants will talk."

"I hadn't thought of that. I mean, I knew it was difficult to hide such a situation, but I hadn't thought about being compelled to offer for the young lady."

"Given that she's so vastly different from the women you normally show interest in, I think she might be very good for you."

Adam's eyes rounded. "Then you're not going to lecture me?"

A smile slowly spread across the burnished planes of Nick's cheek, and he shook his head. "It's time you married."

"I . . . I'm not planning on consummating it."

Nick snickered. "That's the opposite of what I told Fiona when I agreed to wed her."

"You mean even though you were marrying as a *business arrangement*, you desired her?"

"I must have. I didn't think I loved her, but I realize now I've always loved her." He looked up at his younger brother. "I hope you will come to love Miss Hastings. I don't pretend to know her, but I do know she's a decent sort."

Adam was aware of a huge, gnawing void. He wanted what Nick and Lady Fiona had, but that would never happen. Did Nick not know he was serious when he said he'd never love anyone but Maria? In deference to Miss Hastings, he chose not to argue the point. "I think for Miss Hastings' sake, no one else—not even William—needs to know that I've only just met her, that it's not . . . not a love match."

"I agree." Nick turned even more serious than his normal self.

"She will have to petition the Court of Chancery for permission to marry."

"Then she's under age?"

Adam nodded. "And now has no guardian, no living relative. You are close to the Lord Chancellor, are you not?"

"Yes," Nick said. "I'll take care of that. We'll get Devere to be her temporary guardian—since he's family and since Lord Eldon smiles more favorably upon earls, Devere will be an excellent temporary guardian for Miss Hastings. I'll obtain all the necessary approvals tomorrow, with Lord Eldon's help."

For a few moments they were silent, the only noise that of the hissing fire that reflected on Nick's face. Finally Nick turned to him. "Let me ask you this. Did you not find the change in her uncle's will suspicious?"

$\mathcal{C}$hapter 7

"Precisely what I was thinking," Adam said. "Given Miss Hastings' propensity for wailing, I didn't want to bring up the subject until after I could calm her down. But I intend to look into the business."

"Shady dealings, I should say."

"Had Miss Hastings not been there at the solicitor's establishment, I would have torn into him."

"He sounds like a bloody idiot."

"He did let us see the *revised* will."

"I doubt that was ethical."

"She *was* one of the beneficiaries."

Nick shrugged. "I'll give him that."

"Before I bring in old Emmott," Adam said, "I think Miss Hastings and I will poke about the Ceylon Tea Company."

Nick's brows hiked. "Then you're going to share your suspicions with the lady?"

"She may look young—younger than she is—but she's not without intelligence. Once she calms down, she'll begin to question the validity of the new will."

Nick regarded his brother with an amused expression. "Does this mean the bank will be void of your presence for three straight days?"

Adam thought for a moment before he

answered. "I suppose it does. I do have a very capable clerk."

"Does this mean you're not going to get foxed tonight?"

Why was it his older brother always managed to sound like a scolding father when he was only a year older than Adam? "I suppose it does. I may not be in love with Miss Hastings, but I have a new interest, and that is to take care of this young woman."

Nick folded arms across his chest. "Exactly as I said. Miss Hastings will be good for you."

* * *

"Let's begin in the morning room," Lady Fiona said.

Like a glutton with food, Emma devoured all the sensory details which flashed before her on the way to the morning room. Glittering crystal chandeliers, ablaze with hundreds of candles, suspended from heavily decorated ceilings far above. The floor of carrara marble upon which they tread was bordered with sienna marble. The massive arched Palladian windows, pedimented doorways, and gilded pilasters spoke to the classical influences that governed this amazing house.

The morning room—the smallest chamber she'd seen here—was all scarlet and gilt. Even though it was not being used this evening, a fire blazed in the hearth. Everything she saw bespoke the finest quality. The draperies and upholstery were of silk, and she wondered if the gilt cornices over each of the chamber's three windows were of real gold.

And if all these beautiful rooms and all their nearly priceless contents weren't enough to dazzle, the elegant Lady Fiona mesmerized Emma with her melodious voice, fair beauty, and impeccable dress. Emma was compelled to stare at her beautiful hostess. Her flawless face was surrounded by artfully arranged hair of pale blond, and her dress of cerulean blue was surely the most handsome dress Emma had ever beheld. Not only did it fit to perfection, the hand that had sewn the thin muslin gown was also perfect.

Emma found herself wondering if such innate good taste came naturally to those from aristocratic families, or had it come after the lady wed one of the richest men in the kingdom. Adam had told her that his money could make Emma something quite above the ordinary (she most certainly knew herself to be ordinary), but she would never be able to compare favorably with the beauty of Lady Fiona.

When they went back to the home's massive central hall, Emma finally got the opportunity to tilt her head and observe the celestial ceiling.

"Nick brought in an Italian to paint this ceiling," Lady Fiona said.

Emma wondered how the artist had managed to paint such a magnificent scene above his head. Had he lain down? Nymphs and seraphs lazed by a vivid waterfall which sprang from a verdant hill.

The two women then mounted a terrazzo staircase that was wide enough for five to walk abreast. She wondered, too, if its banister was constructed of real gold. The first chamber they came to on the next floor was what Lady Fiona called the Blue Salon. Pale blue silk damask covered the walls, and a thinner silk of the same shade draped the windows, while the furnishings were upholstered in the same blue, only in a heavy silk brocade. All furniture was gilded

French.

"This is lovely," Emma said. It was truly more lovely than any room she had ever seen.

"We spend a great deal of time here, and as you can see, there's room for many people. I will be so happy for you to marry Adam and come play whist with us here. You do play?"

Emma nodded. "I can play, but I will need to gain more experience before I could be truly competitive."

Lady Fiona took Emma's hand, grinning. "Now I must show you our most famous chamber." She led Emma down the corridor lighted by gilded wall sconces and came to a stop in front of a closed door. "This is also the smallest chamber." She opened the door and stood back, beckoning Emma to enter.

A lone candle rested on a slender wall shelf to illuminate a wooden box on the floor. A large white bowl was centered in it.

"This is really the most clever invention," Lady Fiona said. "There's no need for servants here. Fresh water is piped into the bowl, and afterward . . . it's swept away and refilled with clean water."

Emma stared at the contraption for a moment. "A pity it's not a bit higher. It would be awfully difficult to wash one's face in that bowl without contriving to get down on the floor."

Lady Fiona burst into laughter.

Oh, dear, what had Emma said wrong?

"Forgive me for laughing," the lady said, though she made no effort to wipe the smile from her face. "It's just that the notion of one washing one's face in there is funny—though it shouldn't be."

"Pray, my lady, why is it funny? Why should it not be funny? I do not understand."

"I'm sorry. I did not properly explain our water closet." Lady Fiona's ivory cheeks coloured. "One actually sits over the bowl . . ."

All of a sudden, Emma understood. Then she began to laugh at the notion of one washing one's face there. All the while, she nodded. "I do understand. It is a frightfully clever contraption. So you call this a water closet?"

The lady nodded.

"So it's actually a . . . waste eliminator."

"Indeed." Lady Fiona took her hand again. "Permit me to show you our bedchambers. Only family members can see these."

Emma thought each of their set of chambers resembled their owners. Nick's royal blue rooms were masculine, solid, and tasteful. Just like him. And Lady Fiona's ivory chambers exuded her elegance and femininity.

Lady Fiona lingered in her chamber for moment. "Please don't be offended, my dear Emma, but I thought perhaps you might like to wear some of my dresses until yours arrive. I'm sure your lovely muslin dress was perfect for Upper . . .?"

"Barrington."

"But it's not quite smart enough for London. I would, of course, have my maid cut them down for you, since you're smaller than me."

"I couldn't ruin your dresses."

"These would be last year's. I was going to give them away, anyway."

A smile lifted Emma's face. "I've always hated sprigged muslin. I would be delighted to accept your kind offer."

For the next twenty minutes Lady Fiona, along with her maid, showed Emma the dresses, and the maid took her measure. "I will have them ready for you tomorrow."

"Now let's look at the chamber where you'll live until you're officially the next Mrs. Birmingham. It used to be Verity's room. That's Nick's and Adam's only sister. She's now Lady Agar and no longer stays here when she's in London because they have Agar House." Lady Fiona shrugged. "They spend little time in the Capital as they prefer living in Yorkshire."

Verity's old room of emerald green was the only chamber in the house that was devoid of gilt. "It's lovely."

Lady Fiona nodded. "Verity has simple tastes. She's as lovely as this charming room."

From there, they mounted the stairs to the top floor, where Lady Fiona proudly showed Emma the huge turquoise ballroom that took up the entire top floor of their house. "We presented Verity, here. Several hundred attended that night."

Emma would loved to have been there, but only as a spectator, not a participant. She had no desire to participate until she was assured she would not embarrass herself.

They finished up the tour in the library where the brothers had been talking. Both rose when the ladies entered the chamber.

* * *

The bedchamber Lady Fiona assigned to Emma was even more beautiful than the one at Mr. Birmingham's house. It was a swathed in emerald silks—even on the walls—and all the furniture was gilded.

Dear Adam had her portmanteau sent around so she could claim her own necessities. After she dressed in night clothes and climbed upon the big, canopied bed, she had time to reflect on the most important day of her life. It was difficult now to remember the raw hurt that sliced through her when Mr. Wycliff told her she was *not* Uncle Simon's heir, when he'd disclosed Aunt Harriett's death. She'd sat there before the solicitor's desk feeling as if the life had been strangled out of her, unable to utter a single word.

How grateful she had been to Mr. Birmingham . . . *Adam*, she thought reverently, for being her voice.

And how exceedingly grateful she was to him for what came afterward. His stature grew even more when he offered himself as her savior. For that is what he was. Her savior.

The drunken man she'd met the previous night bore no relationship to the commanding, kind-hearted man he was today. Even though she had only known him only four-and-twenty hours, and even though he might be a heathen, she believed she was falling in love with him.

It saddened her to know she would not see him the following day. He would be getting the special license for their marriage and tying up unfinished matters at his bank. Then, she thought with an explosion in her heart, they would marry the next day.

Even were he not vastly rich, she would have been drawn to him. It wasn't just his extraordinary good looks that attracted. It was the man's selflessness and generosity, his altruism. What woman wouldn't fall in love with him?

The day that had begun so badly had turned into the happiest day of her life. What fun it had been to be fitted for beautiful ball gowns, lovely bonnets, and dazzling jewels. She felt like a waif who'd learned she was a princess.

Even the nervousness that had assaulted Emma when she first faced Lady Fiona soon evaporated under that lady's friendly ways. Repeating memories of the day's occurrences prevented Emma from sleeping. Her thoughts dwelt on all of it.

Guilt assailed her, too. Were she truly altruistic, she would not have accepted Adam's offer. But she was far too selfish to deny herself. Instead, she assuaged her conscience by telling herself that marrying her would be good for him. After two consecutive drunken nights, he stayed sober tonight.

She had been able to divert his thoughts from Maria. If only she could purge his mind of that horrid woman!

* * *

As he stood before the altar at St. George's, Miss Hastings' tiny hand in his as she vowed to be his wife, Adam felt as if he were in a dream, a dream steeped in her light rose fragrance. This wasn't how his wedding day was supposed to be. He'd always thought he would marry a beauty with whom he'd fallen in love. Emma was not a beauty (at least she hadn't been when he'd proposed, but she looked quite fetching today). He was not in love with her. And he wasn't even going to bed her.

His tinge of regrets, though, wasn't as strong as his need to take care of Emma. From the first night he'd seen her lugging that giant portmanteau behind her frail little body, he'd felt the need to look after her.

Adam had never been one to sit idly by when he

possessed the capabilities to solve problems. He preferred to lead. In Emma's case, he liked to be the one to make her dreams come true.

When the ceremony was concluded, he and Emma turned around to see Nick and Lady Fiona and William along with Lady Sophia and her brother, Lord Devere, gathered there to celebrate this special occasion. Seeing his family there made the wedding seem real.

He was now a married man. Emma was no longer Miss Hastings. She was now Mrs. Birmingham.

* * *

Adam had lied. His brother William was *not* the most handsome Birmingham brother. But, she had to own, he was very handsome, and just like Adam, he was kind. He and his Lady Sophia, whose beauty Adam had neglected to praise, had insisted on hosting their wedding breakfast, and nothing could have been nicer. Even the flowers— masses of white narcissus—were perfection.

Emma could not have hoped for a better reception from her bridegroom's family. Thankfully, the ivory dress Lady Fiona had cut down for her made a lovely wedding dress. She no longer felt like a waif. In fact, when she peered into her looking glass, she thought no one would take her for the imposter she was. She actually looked as if she belonged in the powerful Birmingham family. (Thought she was not so pretty as the fair Lady Fiona or the dark-haired beauty, Lady Sophia.)

With the addition of Lord Devere, who she learned had been appointed as her temporary guardian, there were seven attending their wedding breakfast in William and Lady Sophia's pale yellow morning room, so she was taken aback when William kept playfully addressing his wife as Isadore. Not wanting to seem too provincial, she refrained from questioning them. She would ask Adam later.

"I am so happy that Adam's wed," Lady Sophia said. "Won't it be great fun for all of us to start our nurseries together?"

Emma diverted her gaze, her cheeks hot.

Adam, too, avoided eye contact with anyone as he directed a great deal of attention to carving up the piece of ham on his porcelain plate.

"My dear wife," William teased, "it is not good manners to speak on such topics. One would think an earl's daughter would not be in such want of good manners."

"You, Mr. Birmingham," Lady Sophia responded lightly, "are not to chide your wife in public. What a shame your pious parents failed to teach you proper manners."

Nick, as the oldest and as was his custom, attempted to preside over the table even if this was not his house. "Enough." He glared at William. "I do miss Verity being here."

"And Mama, too," Adam added, turning to his bride. "Mama is at present in Yorkshire at our sister's home. Verity has been brought to bed of a son."

"The future Earl of Agar," Lady Sophia murmured.

"Perhaps one day, my love," Adam said to Emma, "I will take you up North to meet Verity. None of them spends much time in London."

As Emma sat there with her husband's siblings, it was impossible not to see how deeply in love each of his brothers and their spouses were. "Is she, I wonder, besotted over her husband?" she asked. *Oh, dear.* More heat darted to Emma's cheeks. What a stupid remark. They all must think her a great ninny.

But none of them looked at her as if she'd just broken a fine Sevres vase. In fact, it was as if they understood the transition of her thoughts.

It was her husband who put her at ease. He regarded her with an amused expression as he nodded. "Yes, all of my siblings do act rather besotted over their mates, do they not?"

She nodded shyly.

The two other couples burst out laughing. Lady Sophia brushed a kiss on William's cheek. They were far more demonstrative than stiff Nick and his prim Lady Fiona, but Nick's smoldering gaze when he beheld his wife was more telling than a folio of love poems.

The very contemplation of these couples' love sent her heart racing, her stomach fluttering. *I wish I were truly Adam's wife.*

After the breakfast had been eaten, Adam thanked their hosts. "We must go."

"You did not say where your wedding trip's to be," Lady Fiona said.

Adam shrugged. "Perhaps later we shall travel to the far north to visit Agar and Verity. For now, we stay in London. There is much that demands our attention."

Once they were in his coach, she felt even more exuberant. How thrilled she was to be alone in the coach with him, to have him sitting at her side, holding her hand. "What did you mean *our* attention? You're not racing to get back to that bank of yours?"

"I set my affairs there in order yesterday. What

needs to be done there can be handled by my clerk." He drew a breath. "I thought you and I would pay a visit today at the Ceylon Tea Company."

She peered up at him from beneath lowered brows. "Then you're thinking what I'm thinking?"

He nodded, squeezing her hand. "As husband and wife, we share everything, Emma. All I have is yours. And all your cares are mine. You must feel free to speak with me upon any subject—especially your suspicions about your uncle's will."

"You think there's a chance my uncle's new will was forged?"

"I do."

Her eyes misted, but she was quick to tell him she was not going to cry. "I'm just so touched by your concern for and understanding of . . . me. But before we go to the tea company, I want to show you the last letter Uncle wrote me. A man who wrote that letter could never have cut me off as he did."

"We'll go to our house now and read it."

Our house. It was almost as difficult to believe that gracious mansion her home as it was to think this magnificent man her husband. She did so feel like the waif who found out she was a princess.

$\mathcal{C}$hapter 8

At Adam's house, the staff came rushing into the entry corridor, all starchy and neat, bright smiles on their faces. Studewood bowed to his employer. "I have taken the liberty of assembling the servants to meet the new Mrs. Birmingham."

At first she thought the butler was talking about someone else. It was difficult to think of herself as Mrs. Birmingham, and equally difficult to imagine herself as mistress of this magnificent house. How touched she was that Adam, with all the duties he'd had to discharge in the past four-and-twenty hours, had thought to notify the servants of his nuptials.

She duly faced each of the nine servants and inclined her head as they were introduced, as each of them curtsied to her. She would endeavor to remember each of their names.

"Now, my love," Adam said, proffering his arm, "it's time I give you a proper tour of your new home."

My new home. She could barely credit it. As happy as she was, she feared someone would come tap her on the shoulder and tell her it had all been a mistake and she must return to Upper Barrington.

During her previous stay here she'd only been able to briefly gawk at this splendid house. Now she would be able to take as long as she liked to peruse each room. The ground floor was of little interest. It housed the usual porter's room and morning room. From there they climbed up the richly banistered staircase to the floor that had been calculated to dazzle the visitor. The huge drawing room she had so reluctantly been whisked past that first night brought her to an abrupt halt. She was compelled to merely stand there in awe of its beauty.

Everything in the, yes, *opulentacious,* chamber was palace-worthy from the elegant richly cut, soft green velvet sofas in the French style, to the fine silk draperies in hues of the rising sun, to the Administer carpets which picked up the design on the wainscoting of the lower wall. Huge, multi-tiered chandeliers hung from the ceiling far above.

But the most mesmerizing item in chamber was a large portrait of a beautiful woman which hung over the chimneypiece.

Maria.

She wanted to ask if Maria was the beauty, but she didn't want to have her suspicion confirmed. Who could ever compete with such an incomparable woman? The woman in the portrait was possessed of dark hair, creamy skin, and a voluptuous figure. All assets that Emma lacked.

She was too curious to remain silent. Never removing her gaze from the portrait, she strove for a casual voice when she asked, "Is that Maria?" She held her breath. Why had she permitted that horrid Maria to intrude on her own wedding day.

He shook his head. "No, that's a young Lady Hamilton. Romney was obsessed with her youthful beauty."

"Romney? And Lady Hamilton? This must have

cost a fortune!"

He chuckled. "You're right. The bidding was very steep." He refrained from reminding her how wealthy a man she had married.

She drew a deep breath and once more attempted to adopt a casual attitude. "So, do you have a portrait of Maria?" Truth be told, her curiosity to see her rival was eating at her like a corrosive acid.

"I regret I never thought to have her sit," he said somberly.

His words and the melancholy manner in which they were spoken wounded her. Emma did not know if it was good or bad that he hadn't thought to have Maria's portrait painted. Did that mean he'd thought of Maria as a disposable mistress for much of their affair? Or did it mean he didn't need her portrait because he never planned to be away from her? She eyed the Romney and changed the subject. "So this was painted before she was Lady Hamilton?"

"Yes. I believe she was then known as Emma Hart the Tart."

"How uncharitable!"

"I shouldn't have spoken in such a manner in front of you. A maiden."

She moved to him, placed a gentle hand on his sleeve, and lowered her voice, aiming for something sultry. "You forget, sir, I am now a married woman." Her heart pounding furiously, she gazed into his black eyes, took in the strong planes of his handsome face and was breathtakingly cognizant of how close they were, of the warmth of his flesh, the way he towered over her like a knight protector. Which, indeed, he was to her.

Striving for sultry had not succeeded. He merely turned away. "Well, now, allow me to show you the dinner room."

She latched onto his arm as they strode past the stairwell that was lighted from a huge glass dome on the house's roof.

The dinner room was not large, no doubt owing to the necessary narrowness of town houses (unless one had a huge, landed property on Piccadilly, as did Nicholas Birmingham). The mahogany table here could not accommodate more than a dozen—unlike Sir Arthur's huge dining chamber at his country house, which could handily seat four-and-twenty. The large fireplace here centered the chamber, and because the room was not vast, she suspected dining here would be wonderfully cozy and warm. Especially on winter nights.

He came to stand beside her, setting his arm about her shoulder. "Now that I am a married man, we shall have to host dinner parties."

She look up at him and smiled. "How fun." In truth, she was terrified of planning and presiding over a dinner party. She was but twenty years old and green in the ways of the *ton.* But she had no intentions of letting Adam know of her insecurities. She would do everything in her power to be the best wife a man could have. She vowed to make herself capable in every way.

He turned to her. It was as if he were reading her thoughts. "Don't be alarmed. I realize you know no one in London at present, save for my brothers and their wives. I promise you, that will change. With Ladies Fiona and Sophia guiding you, you'll soon be the toast of the Capital."

She doubted that. Even with Adam's money

and all the finery he bought for her she would never be as remarkable as either of her beautiful sisters-in-law.

Next, he led her up the last flight of stairs. "I hope you'll be satisfied with your apartments."

Her brows hiked. "More than one room?"

He smiled and nodded. "The previous owners, Lord and Lady Albuthnot, took the whole floor for their apartments—save for the chamber where you slept the other night. They had no children, and they hosted guests only at their country house.

Wideacres. She'd read in the society pages of Lord and Lady Albuthnot's lavish country estate in Warwickshire.

"No wonder the house is so magnificent! The Albuthnots are famed as arbiters of good taste." Then she paused. "That's not to say the Birminghams aren't also. Now that I've seen all three brothers' homes, I know it would be impossible to surpass them in elegance—not that I hold myself up as an expert!"

A tender expression on his face, he paused on the stairway and looked down at her. "I saw your selections in clothing and jewels. You, my dear wife, are possessed of an unerring eye."

She felt lighter than air. *My dear wife.* Even if his words weren't heart-felt, the very notion of being *his* dear wife was enough to push her to the verge of swooning.

"Where are the servants' chambers?"

"The top floor. It's accessible by a narrower staircase off the scullery."

There was something so intimate about having a man show her to her bedchamber.

Her heart started hammering as they strolled

along the wooden corridor to her apartments. She stood silently as he opened the door, then she followed him into the fine rose-coloured room. He turned to her and drew her hands into his. "This suite of rooms belongs to the mistress of the house, and that is you, Mrs. Birmingham."

As happy as it made her to be Mrs. Birmingham, it made her even happier to feel his hands tenderly clasping hers. Two days ago had been the most exciting day of her life (except for the sad news of her uncle and aunt's deaths, of course). Today was the happiest day of her twenty years.

"I'm very grateful to you, Mr. . . . Adam. I pray you will never regret this day, that one day I will be able to repay you in some way."

He smiled. "My repayment will be your happiness."

"Then, sir, consider yourself repaid a hundredfold."

He kissed her hand and dropped it as his gaze circled the chamber. "Now let me show you your rooms."

The first thing she saw was her banged-up portmanteau. It looked out of place in the perfection of this beautiful chamber. *Perfection.* It was a word she was beginning to associate with everything the Birminghams touched. Even though her experience in stately homes was limited to Sir Arthur's and to Fleur House, a stately home near Upper Barrington which belonged to a wealthy brewer, she knew that everything about the three Birmingham houses she'd seen was not only of the best quality and in pristine upkeep, but all three glorified residences housed only the finest in furnishings, carpets, art, silver, and porcelains. She had even spotted a Holbein at William and Sophia's exquisite home. The lavish use of fine silks in draperies, wall coverings and upholstery impressed her as much as anything for she well knew the prohibitive cost of silk. Sir Arthur's and Fleur House both used lesser fabrics.

The paper on her chamber's wall was sprigged with soft rouge-coloured roses, the colour matching that on the draperies and bedcovering. She wanted to take in every detail of this beautiful room but must follow her husband as he was taking her to see the mistress's study in the adjacent chamber.

She paused in the study's doorway and gaped. "This room is just for me?" Centered upon a pale pink Aubusson carpet stood a fine gilt escritoire, and all the writing implements awaited her.

"Indeed."

She sighed. "I shall spend a great deal of time here."

"You know that many people with whom to correspond?"

"I love the idea of having my own writing room so much, I shall have to write letters to everyone I've ever known." She giggled. "Be assured I shall sign them all *Mrs. Birmingham.* I do fancy that name." She did not know what possessed her, but she turned and eyed him. "As I fancy you."

Her words obviously embarrassed him. "Heigh ho, it's time to show you your dressing room. You will, of course, need a lady's maid."

She started to protest. She'd gotten along very well dressing herself for twenty years. But she did not want to be an embarrassment to him. Nor did she want to embarrass herself by admitting to the deficiencies in her toilette. "How does one go about selecting a lady's maid?"

"We'll ask Lady Sophia. She knows everyone. She'll be able to select one for you."

Her gaze fanned over the feminine dressing room. Two pieces of furniture dominated it: a gilt and ivory clothes press and a gilded settee covered in more of the rose-coloured silk, this a brocade. "It's lovely."

"Well there, now that you've seen your chambers, I suppose you should find that letter of your uncle's."

She went back to the bedchamber, suddenly conscious of the huge bed with each of its four posters anchoring thick velvet curtains of the same rose. Being in the chamber with him and realizing that most married couples would share a bed brought heat to her cheeks. Her cheeks weren't the only part of her reacting to the thought. A strange stirring settled low in her torso. It made her feel breathless and lightheaded.

Was something wrong with her? She had never experienced anything like it before.

In her portmanteau she found Uncle's letter and handed it to Adam.

He unfolded it and began to read.

My Dear Niece,

As I am now in my sixth decade, I lament that I've never married, that I have no children of my own to carry on my life's work. But I am satisfied that my brother's only child, my dear niece, being of a moldable age, can be groomed to continue all that I've begun, now and long after I've departed this earth.

I wouldn't be so presumptuous had you not repeatedly conveyed to me how much you are lured by the Capital. Also, your great aunt has so kindly and frequently written to me, praising your abilities. She has consistently boasted upon your intelligence and remarked on your maturity that exceeds your chronological years. Those are qualities your father —may my dear brother rest in peace—possessed in abundance. Here at the Ceylon Tea Company I am surrounded by those of lesser intelligence and will look forward to being in your good company. A pity your father could not live to see you. I did promise him I would look after you. And now the time has come.

The remainder of the letter dealt with making travel arrangements for her journey to London. Adam handed it back to her. "Something's rotten in Denmark."

She scrunched up her nose. "At the Ceylon Tea Company, more likely."

He proffered his arm. "I suggest we investigate, Mrs. Birmingham."

* * *

Twenty minutes into their coach ride she spotted the familiar George inn. She had, after all, spent more non-sleeping hours there than anywhere in London. How different it looked in the mid-day sun than it had looked the day she'd spent hours waiting there for her poor uncle.

Her breath caught when just a short distance away she spotted the green and gold sign of the Ceylon Tea Company. A strange, morbid emptiness gnawed at her when she realized how very close Uncle Simon would have been to the posting inn where she'd arrived. If he'd been alive.

He could have walked to greet her when she disembarked. If he'd been alive. Seeing the short distance between the two awakened her to her uncle's thought processes, to his (she hoped) happy anticipation of her visit.

Such a little thing to make her so vastly melancholy. Such a little thing to emphasize his loss more even than seeing his last will and testament.

The company's building was much larger than she had expected. It took up an entire block and was comprised of warehouses on the ground floor and the floor above it. Offices were located on the top floor. As they climbed the stairs to the offices, she tried to recall the name of Uncle Simon's business partner. "As young men who'd been shareholders of the East India Trading Company," she explained, "my uncle and his associate established the business thirty years ago."

"I didn't realize your uncle had a partner."

"I do wish I could recall his name," she said with a sigh.

They were soon to learn, for upon entering the top floor, the first thing a visitor saw was a pair of large offices. One had a large sign on the door reading Simon Hastings, Proprietor. The other, Harold Faukes, Proprietor.

Between the two offices was a desk occupied by a bespectacled, red-headed clerk. She wondered if this could be Ashburnham. Should they ask to speak to Mr. Faukes or to Mr. Ashburnham?

She did not have to decide. Adam spoke. "I should like to speak to Mr. Faukes," he said to the clerk.

"May I say who's calling?" the clerk asked in a non-cultured voice. She studied the young man.

The sleeves of his woolen jacket nearly covered his hands. It must have come from one of the second-hand shops she'd been told were plentiful in London.

"Mr. and Mrs. Birmingham."

The clerk's eyes widened. "Mr. Faukes' banker?"

"Indeed."

The clerk went into the office. His desk was stacked with shipping labels, including one he'd just addressed.

"So you really are his banker?" she asked her husband, surprised.

He nodded. "I just this minute realized it. Surprisingly, I was *not* your uncle's."

Mr. Ashburnham returned, eyeing her husband. "Mr. Faukes will see you now."

As they swept past the clerk, Adam casually asked, "And you are?"

"James Ashburnham, sir."

Her stomach lurched. She knew they lived in a society where men were innocent until proven guilty, but she instinctively believed this man guilty of significant fraud.

In Mr. Faukes' office, the man rose and greeted Adam, ignoring her. "Mr. Birmingham, what an unexpected pleasure. What brings you to my humble establishment?"

Adam looked from him to Emma. "My wife. May I present Mrs. Birmingham, the former Emma Hastings, niece of your late business partner?"

Mr. Faukes looked taken aback for a moment, then his face sombered. "Allow me to say how bereft we all are over your uncle's sad passing." He inclined his head. "Please accept my deepest sympathy."

She nodded morosely.

He then smiled upon her and asked that they be seated. "What a pleasure it is to meet you. Your uncle had been looking forward to your visit." He gave Adam a puzzled look. "I had not known there was connection between you and Simon's niece."

"We've only just married."

"Then I daresay she's not too distressed over Simon's new will. Your wife will never lack for money now that she's a Birmingham, begging your pardon for bringing up such a subject."

"My wife was indeed aggrieved over the terms of her uncle's will. She was led to believe Mr. Hastings wished to groom her to relieve him of some of his duties."

"It is my opinion," she said shyly, "that Uncle Simon wished to see the world during his later years. . ." Her voice trailed off. Tears sprang to her eyes, tears for Uncle Simon and the dreams he had never been able to achieve. She managed to control herself from dissolving into a watering pot.

"I'm not surprised. He loved to talk about the world. He'd always wanted to see India." Mr. Faukes grew solemn. "Such a pity. He was in the prime of his life. I don't need to tell you how much I miss him. We met when he was but nineteen, and I was one-and-twenty. We accomplished many of our dreams."

"Did Mr. Hastings tell you he intended to leave his share of the company to Mr. Ashburnham?" Adam asked.

Mr. Faukes shrugged, his lips pursed. "It was my impression as of late that he intended to leave everything to Miss Hastings, er, Mrs. Birmingham."

Adam nodded pensively. "Can you think of

anything that would have changed his mind?"

Mr. Faukes thought for a moment, shaking his head. "Not to my knowledge."

"He was close to Ashburnham?" Adam asked.

"We're both close to him. We work together six days a week, and he's capable for one not of the highest intelligence."

That would explain the comment in Uncle Simon's letter about stupid people.

"Let me ask you this," Adam said. "Can you tell me who Jonathan Booker and Sidney Wolf are?"

Mr. Faukes' brows dipped as he appeared deep in contemplation. Then he slowly shook his head.

Adam expressed his thanks to Mr. Faukes and left. To her surprise, he choose not to interview James Ashburnham.

Once they had returned to the carriage, she asked, "Who are Jonathan Booker and Sidney Wolf?"

"The two witnesses to your uncle's will."

$\mathcal{C}$hapter 9

"Where are we going?" his wife asked.

"To my solicitor's." He felt guilty that his obsession to investigate Hastings' will was keeping him from showing his bride the delights of London.

"For his advice on Uncle's will?"

"Yes." He peered from the window, glad they were ensconced in the coach on this blustery, gray day. At least it wasn't raining.

"Are you sure it's permissible for you to spend so much time away from your business?"

A smile eased across his face. "This is, after all, my honeymoon. Am I not entitled to time off from work?" He clasped her hand. "*Our* honeymoon. And I mean to show you some of London's sights. Tell me a place that holds allure for you."

She considered his question for a moment. "I should like to see Westminster Abbey."

Her response surprised him. "What is it about the place that appeals to you?"

She giggled. "Because I have an active imagination, I will be able to stand in the nave while my mind conjures a vision of kings' lavish coronations. I'll fancy myself one of those coronet-wearing peeresses who have a clear view of the sovereign slowly moving toward the altar, long robes flowing behind him, then departing the same route with an enormous crown on the royal head.

"And there's a maudlin streak in me that has always sought to see where the country's great statesmen and authors are buried. Ridiculous, I know."

"Not at all. Now for my confession." He paused as she looked up anxiously. "I've never been to Westminster Abbey. Your description has now kindled my desire to go there."

Since they had wed he'd taken up the practice of sitting next to her rather than across from her in the carriage. It was not at all unpleasant. He attributed the pleasant sensation to the light rose scent he had come to associate with her.

They crossed the Thames and before long were back in Holborn. His solicitor, Donald Emmott, did business in a building not more than a three-minute drive from Wycliff's establishment.

At Emmott's place of business, Adam and Emma disembarked and entered the building. In spite of the many years Emmott had worked for Adam and his brothers, this was the first time one of them had ever come here. When men were as wealthy as the Birminghams, those in their employ always came to them.

Adam's late father, who was the shrewdest man he'd ever known—despite *not* being a gentleman—had selected Emmott many years ago, and the solicitor's professionalism could not be surpassed.

As soon as Adam announced himself to Emmott's clerk, the solicitor fairly flew from his office to greet him. (Actually a man of Emmott's advanced years did not exactly fly, but he hobbled at a fast clip.)

Though the man must be close to eighty, his

voice was strong and clear when he greeted Adam. Smiling broadly, he then turned to Emma. "And this young lady must be your lovely bride. I am, indeed, honored that Mr. and Mrs. Adam Birmingham have entered my establishment."

"Thank you, sir, for the friendly greeting," Adam said. "There's a matter regarding my wife's relative that we wish to ask you about."

"Please come into my office."

Unlike Wycliff, Adam's solicitor did not put a large desk between him and his clients. Emmott sat on an armchair near a cozy velvet sofa and invited the newlyweds to sit on the sofa. "Now what is the problem?" he asked. His white eyebrows dipped in concern.

Adam showed him Emma's letter from her uncle, explained that the uncle died before she arrived, and revealed his suspicions about the new will.

Emmott placed spectacles on his nose and quickly looked over it. Eyeing Emma, he asked, "May I keep this for a short time?"

She nodded her consent.

The solicitor then regarded Adam. "I believe you have every right to be skeptical. In fact, I'm shocked over Wycliff's unprofessionalism. If one of my *living* clients sent me a new will, I would demand they do it over under my supervision. Home-made wills are too easy to break."

"Break?" Emma asked. "Do you mean I can challenge the new will?"

"Indeed you can," Emmott said.

"Then will you?" Adam asked the solicitor.

"I will immediately. The challenge will have to be done in Miss, er, Mrs. Birmingham's name."

Adam was relieved. "I was hoping this was

something you'd be able to do. We'd prefer that the so-called new owner not take possession of my wife's uncle's house."

She nodded. "It's next door to us."

"I wouldn't want a scoundrel living next door to me, either," the solicitor said.

"We don't *know* he's a scoundrel," she offered.

Adam was not as charitable as his wife.

Emmott stood. "Allow me to get your signature on some papers, Mrs. Birmingham. It will take a moment to prepare the documents."

Ten minutes later, Adam and his wife were ready to leave when Emmott said, "I have worked with a man who's an expert in detecting forged handwriting. I want him to compare your uncle's letter to the new will."

Adam pursed his lips. "I would like to see some samples of Ashburnham's handwriting to compare also. Perhaps I'll place a large order for Ceylon Tea."

Emmott nodded. "If Ashburnham's hand is the same which prepared the new will, our Mr. Coyle will most certainly be able to determine that."

"I had no idea there was such a thing as a handwriting expert," Emma said.

"It's yet to stand up in court, to my knowledge, but it can be most helpful in ferreting out fraud."

"What's next?" Adam asked.

"Since I am acquainted with Wycliff, I'm going to go around to his establishment, explain that I've been retained by Mr. and Mrs. Birmingham, and ask to see the new will."

Adam thanked him, shook his hand, and left.

When they returned to the carriage, he directed the coachman to take them to Westminster Abbey, then turned to his wife. "How did you like

Emmott?"

She frowned. "I wish Uncle Simon had employed him instead of Mr. Wycliff—not that Mr. Wycliff did not seem to be very nice."

What a sweet nature his Emma possessed. *His?* Why did he think on this woman he barely knew as *his*? Granted, he did seem to have taken her under his care in much the same way one did a lost puppy. And, according to the law, she was now his. How daunting.

He settled against the seat back. "Now, my dear wife, I begin your exploration of London with a visit to Westminster Abbey."

She seemed impossibly young as she looked up at him, not at all like a woman who would attain her majority within a year. "Just riding along in your coach, taking in the sights and sounds of the Capital is amusement enough for me. I could never, ever tire of London. It's the most exhilarating place on earth, is it not?"

"I have little basis for comparison, but I believe you're right. At least that's what I am told. My brother William has traveled to every European capital, and he assures me that nothing compares to London in every respect, particularly in its vastness."

She sighed. "I wonder if I'll ever know my way around."

He squeezed her hand. "You won't need to. You will always have a skilled coachman at your beck and call."

A look of admiration swept across her sweet little face. "Because I've had the good fortune to wed the wealthy Mr. Birmingham."

It had always been his fear that a woman would marry him for his fortune. That was most undoubtedly the case at present, but it no longer mattered to him. It wasn't as if it were to be a *real* marriage. It wasn't as if he were going to fall in love with her. He was happy his fortune would help her achieve her dreams. Lord knows his dreams had been snuffed when Maria left him. He fleetingly thought of Maria's beauty, of her angel-like voice when she sung arias. He tried to recall any plans he'd ever had of making her his wife. Unaccountably, it had never crossed his mind to marry her. Even though he loved her very much. Was that Nick's influence? Nick had always stressed that gentlemen did not marry women like Maria.

Even in the early days of their love affair, he had been aware that Maria had taken many lovers before him. It hadn't bothered the callow youth he'd been. He'd rather fancied being with an experienced woman to polish off his . . . accomplishments. Now he was startlingly aware of her matrimonial ineligibility. And it bothered him. Because now he didn't care. He only wanted her back. Even if she *had* wed her Italian nobleman.

If she were to return now and beg his forgiveness, he would not only forgive her, he would marry her without a moment's hesitation.

Then he suddenly realized he would never be able to marry Maria. He was a married man. Even though Emma did not love him, he could not reject her. She was like an abused pup for whom he felt solely responsible.

He could not deny Emma evoked tender feelings in him. Not romantic feelings. Just tender feelings.

By the time they reached at Westminster Abbey he was mired in a morose mood. That she acted like an excited child, flitting from one section to the other, helped him shed his foul humor. He had thought she might be drawn to Poet's Corner, but the final resting place that mesmerized her the most was the plot where Pitt the Younger was buried. She stood there, observing it, a solemn look upon her face. "Our country's youngest-ever leader. How remarkable," she said somberly. "How tragic that he died in office at such a young age."

Adam swallowed. "Only six-and-forty. It was amazing that he took the highest office in the British Isles at the tender age of four-and-twenty."

She nodded. "I remember when he died, my Aunt Harriett cried. I had never before seen my aunt cry. In fact, I had never before seen her show emotion."

He frowned. "She must have been a Tory."

She whirled at him. "Whether he was a Tory or a Whig does not signify, sir. He was our country's leader, and his death left a huge void."

He held up a flattened palm. "I'm not arguing with you. It just so happens that the Birminghams have always supported Whigs. In fact, Nick has been persuaded by our brother-in-law, Lord Agar, to stand for Parliament as a Whig."

A huge smile brightened her face. "Capital! It's thrilling to think I shall be related, by marriage, to a Member of Parliament. We must help in his electioneering."

"All of us plan to. See, another good reason for me to marry. One more person to get behind my brother's candidacy."

"At least he has the fortune to wage a good campaign."

Adam nodded. "And Agar has always controlled

the seat in Doncaster."

He moved to stand by the tomb of Charles James Fox.

"I really think the colonists have done this electioneering thing better than us," she said. "In their country, a man must represent the geographical area in which he lives. It's really quite silly that Nick will represent a district hundreds of miles from his home."

He was surprised—pleasantly so—that this young woman knew so much about political theory. The opinion she'd just voiced happened to echo his own. But that in no way diminished his desire to see Nick representing Newcastle in the House of Commons.

He nodded. "Perhaps one day our leaders will become enlightened."

Her gaze dropped to the final resting place of Charles James Fox. "Such a pity that two of our greatest statesmen ever died the same year."

"Yes," she agreed, her voice solemn. "At the time I felt as if a dark cloud hung over our country. I thought we would never again prosper, never again be led by such able leaders."

She placed a dainty gloved hand on his sleeve and spoke softly. "But time marches on, and fears subside, do they not?"

"They do."

"As does heartache," she said in a gentle voice that was barely audible.

He wished to God people would quit telling him he'd soon be over the broken heart Maria had inflicted upon him. That just could not be. No woman would ever again own his heart.

"I'm in such awe," she said excitedly. "To think I'm standing in the very place where centuries worth of kings have been crowned. I daresay this building looks much as it did during medieval times."

Having spent most of his life in London, he was seeing the metropolis with fresh eyes. This young woman was giving him a renewed appreciation of the city of his birth. He'd never realized how fortunate he was to live in a huge, diversified city in which so much significant history had left its mark.

"Tell me," she said. "Have you always lived in the Capital?"

He shrugged. "Once my father's fortune was secured, he purchased the requisite country estate. We went there a few times a year, though our principal residence was in London. South of the River Thames."

"That is not in the fashionable area, is it?"

"Not at all."

"Does your mother still live there?"

He shook his head. "My mother prefers the country. When she's not visiting her children — each of us maintains rooms for her—she lives at Great Acres."

He took her hand. "You've now met three of her four offspring. We were all raised to mimic the higher classes, according to my father's wishes. Our parents were . . . are . . . not of the same upbringing. I am preparing you for meeting my mother. Her voice is not cultured. She is far removed from what her children were created to be. She's not even Church of England!"

"I'm sure I will love her—even if she is an atheist."

He chuckled. "She's not an atheist—quite the opposite. She's a Methodist."

"Then you were raised a Christian?" A look of incredulity swept across her face.

"I hate to disavow your misconception about me—though I do confess that as an adult I've relaxed my religious fervor."

She let out an audible swish of her lungs. "I am happy you are not an atheist. "

"I beg you not say anything to my mother about my . . . infrequent church going. She is still having a difficult time accepting that her children are all Church of England." He gave a mock shudder. "Mama is exceedingly stern and terribly religious."

She smiled. "I believe, sir, you must be describing my Aunt Harriett! Though my aunt used the most pompous upper-class accent and would never attend a service that was not Church of England."

"I must not be nearly as charitable as you for I cannot say *I'm sure I would have loved your aunt.*"

She giggled. "If I didn't owe her so much for raising me when I became orphaned, I probably wouldn't have loved her either. Sadly, I am probably the only living person who ever had tender feelings for my exceedingly stern aunt."

His brows lowered. "How did our conversation move to such topics?"

"I asked if you'd always lived in London."

She was blessed with a remarkable memory. "So you did." He offered his arm. "Have you seen enough?"

"I think so. It's not as if we can't come back." She stopped in her stride and looked up at him. "Though I know I will not normally be able to hoard your precious time."

He patted her hand. "I enjoy showing you London. You are aware of Dr. Johnson's remark about our city?"

She nodded. "*When a man is tired of London, he is tired of life.*"

She must be well read, too. "I suppose one has little to do in Upper Barrington other than reading."

"Provided one can get one's hands on great books. We have no lending library there, and the price of new books is steep. Fortunately, Sir Arthur allows me free use of his library."

"Then I daresay you've been subjected to tomes by long-dead Romans and Greeks."

"How right you are!"

"Where would you like to go next?" he asked as they moved out into the windy day.

"Do you suppose we could ride in Hyde Park?"

"We could, but it will be sparsely populated on so gray a day." And he would much rather display his new wife there *after* her fashionable new dresses were delivered. At least they would be inside a closed carriage today.

"I should still like to see it. If I knew anyone, I should be most woefully anxious to show off my handsome new husband."

Handsome new husband? He was never comfortable when hearing himself described as handsome. Nor was he comfortable being this woman's husband. Things had happened so quickly he had a difficult time adjusting to being a married man, to putting another's welfare over his own. He'd always been exceedingly selfish.

For Emma's sake, he hoped he did not revert to his former self. She had no one else in this huge, strange city.

Chapter 10

Their trip through Hyde Park was cut short when the skies erupted. Emma's disappointment vanished the moment she walked into their house and Studewood informed her that Madame De Guerney had delivered her new dresses. "Two carriages were full of the lovely gowns. I've taken the liberty of delivering them to Mrs. Birmingham's chambers. A pity there's no maid to deal with them."

"It's only a matter of time before my wife gets her own maid," Adam said.

She turned to her husband. "Oh, you must come and see, Adam! You must tell me which you prefer me to wear to dinner tonight."

He offered his arm as they mounted the stairs. She was reminded of the first time she had climbed these stairs with him, and it had been she who had taken his arm in an attempt to steady him, fearing the inebriated man would tumble down the stairs. Thank God he was no longer that man.

When they strolled into her bedchamber and she saw the two stacks of elegant gowns piled upon her bed, she gasped. "They're all so beautiful! I cannot believe they're to be mine."

"You need to become accustomed to having beautiful things." He moved closer and set a gentle hand on her shoulder.

"Which should you like me to wear to dinner?"

"The pale blue. Tomorrow night I shall take you to the theatre. Then you must wear the lavender gown with your amethyst and diamond necklace. "

The one that had been owned by a member of the Bourbon royal family. Even with the magnificent necklace and the beautiful gown, she worried she would look like a dowdy imposter. She had no talent in dressing hair. And there was the fact she was quite plain.

A rap sounded at her door. "Come in," Adam said.

Studewood entered the chamber, trailed by a girl who looked no more than sixteen. "Lady Sophia has sent this young female to be your maid." He looked at the girl. "I'll have you tell Mrs. Birmingham about your qualifications." He then eyed Emma. "If madam isn't satisfied, there will be other candidates." He turned and left the chamber.

Adam began to move toward the door."Since this is a lady's discussion, I'll be in my library, dear one."

Emma invited the girl to sit beside her on the settee. "Now, tell me about yourself." The girl could not have been in service for very long. She was so young.

"My name is Therese." She spoke English with a heavy French accent. "The truth is that I have not yet taken a position as a lady's maid, but my sister she is maid to Lady Maryann, who is sister to Lady Sophia, who is, I am told, some kind of sister to you."

Emma nodded. Were French maids not the most desired?

"My sister is very capable, and she has trained me. I will take care of your . . ." Her gaze went to the pile of dresses on the bed. "Your beautiful dresses, and I am told that I have the gift of dressing madame's hair."

Despite Studewood's warning, Emma's intuition told her she could do no better than to engage Therese. "That is exactly what I need. Do you suppose you could start today?"

* * *

When his wife entered the dinner room, he stood as he always did when a female entered a chamber, but this time he was stunned at how truly lovely Emma looked. He'd been telling her that she would be the toast of the *ton*, but he hadn't really thought she would be *this* striking. Of course, she was not a radiant beauty like Maria, but she would most certainly draw attention. His lazy gaze went from her swept up hair, along her sweet face, down her graceful neck to the soft swell of breasts. His breath hitched. "You're more beautiful than I thought possible."

He walked toward her, set his hand to her waist, and guided her to her chair. "I take it you engaged the maid?"

She lowered herself into the chair to which he had led her. "I did, and I'm very pleased with her."

"As am I."

As he dined on clear turtle soup, followed by turbot, he kept staring at her. It was as if she were a different person. She was the same Emma, yet she wasn't. Dressed so elegantly, she now easily looked her age, looked like a privileged young matron. As pleased as he was, a part of him mourned for the loss of that girl in the sprigged muslin dress.

When he'd offered her marriage, he thought only of making a hysterical young woman happy. He had been pleased it was within his power to brighten her life. Now, though, he realized she looked like a wife who would bring him credit. Women would embrace friendship with one so wholesome looking. Men would admire her fine good looks.

Part of his attraction to Maria had been the pride that strummed through him when men looked hungrily at her. She'd been like a prized race horse—which somewhat shamed him now. Nevertheless, he was looking forward to sitting in his box tomorrow night, knowing that all eyes would be on his lovely wife.

"What are your plans for tomorrow?" she asked.

"I thought we'd return to Wycliff's in the morning."

She nodded. "And in the afternoon?"

"Would you like to go to the British Museum?

Her smile was as radiant as the chandelier that hung above their table. "Indeed I would."

* * *

Therese helped her into her night shift, then after bidding her mistress good night, took Emma's lovely new dress away to care for it.

In bed, Emma had a difficult time falling asleep. She kept remembering how Adam had stared at her when she had walked into the dinner room. For the first time in her life, she had felt like a woman. She'd been flattered when he'd said she was beautiful. It was an exaggeration, of course, but she'd actually felt like a great beauty as she sat beside him and felt his eyes continuing to peruse the new Emma.

Lying in the bed so close to her husband's

bedchamber made her startlingly aware of what an empty marriage theirs was. She felt guilty for her melancholy thoughts. It wasn't as if she wasn't grateful to him. Because of his kindness, she had a lovely home, beautiful gowns and jewels—and London. Those things should make her very happy. She *was* happy, happier than she'd ever been, but that one omission—his love— kept her from enjoying perfect happiness.

Not that she deserved perfect happiness. She did not deserve any of these wondrous things. She'd done nothing to deserve them. It wasn't even as if she were a great beauty he should like to hang on his arm.

Her thoughts tangled in her mind and kept her from sleeping. She found herself wondering if she and Adam would ever have children. Then, quite naturally, she wondered if Adam would ever share her bed. The very thought spiked her pulse. Which kept her awake for a considerable period of time.

* * *

Therese had opened the draperies in Emma's bedchamber to fill the room with brilliant sunlight. Emma was surprised she had slept so late. But, of course, it was near dawn before sleep finally fell over her.

Because of the sunshine, it was impossible to be melancholy this morning. She sat in her bed propped up on mounds of pillows, sipping her hot chocolate. Aunt Harriett would have been mortified at her indolence, but Emma felt as if she were in an intoxicating dream. Everything was so wondrous. Never would she have thought to have so beautiful a bedchamber, to be mistress of so fine a home, to be wife to the most perfect of beings. (For she believed he must have conquered his sottishness.) Her heart expanded at the thought of Adam.

How he had changed from the night she had met him. He'd been so witless she never would have thought him a capable man. But sober, he exuded intelligence and leadership. One quality that endeared him to her the most had been present on the night they met and had only strengthened since: his kindness.

Even that first night, so drunk he could hardly find his way home, he'd been compassionate toward her, a strange young woman lugging a portmanteau in the rain.

Her thoughts flitted to what she would wear today. She wanted to look so pretty he would forget that wretched Maria.

Therese entered her sunlit chamber, this time carrying a soft yellow morning dress. "Has madame finished her chocolate?"

Emma nodded, set her tray aside, and leapt from the bed. "I wish for you to make me lovely. I must dazzle my husband."

* * *

"Mr. Wycliff," Adam said, "my wife and I shall need a list of all those employed in Mr. Hastings' household."

"It won't take me a moment to get you that information. Is there anything else I can procure for you?"

Adam felt like asking him to throw out the bogus will, but he had confidence the truth would prevail. "That will be quite enough."

A few minutes later, a neat list of Simon Hastings' domestic staff was handed to him.

Wycliff cleared his throat. "I am sure you are aware that your own solicitor, Mr. Emmott, has met with me?"

"Yes, of course."

Wycliff's gaze shifted to Emma. "Rest assured, Mrs. Birmingham, your uncle's property will not be handed over to anyone until this situation is resolved."

"Thank you, Mr. Wycliff."

They left the solicitor's chambers, and once they were in the coach, she turned to Adam. "I didn't know you were going to ask for those names. What is the purpose? Are we going to try to interview each of them?"

He shook his head. "I was looking for the names Jonathan Booker and Sydney Wolf."

"The witnesses to Uncle's will."

"Wouldn't it have been the most natural thing for your uncle to have his servants act as witnesses?"

"Indeed it would."

"He didn't. None of the servants bear those names."

"Oh, dear."

"By the way, I've indirectly placed a large order for Ceylon Tea."

"To see James Ashburnham's handwriting?"

He nodded.

"You used your own name?"

"No. The order was actually placed by one of the businesses I own."

"You own other businesses beside the bank?"

"I'm one of the shareholders in a company that acquires choice properties. I like owning land. *We* like owning land. My brothers are also shareholders."

She giggled. "I daresay none of the Birminghams will have to buy tea anytime during

the next year." They had ordered half a dozen
cases.

Their coach turned onto The Strand, where it
was going to be difficult to progress because of all
the conveyances making their way along one of
the Capital's busiest streets. From his window,
the passing vehicles varied from a cart piled high
with potatoes to an aggressive hackney driver
trying to weave in and out of the snarl, various
tilburies and phaetons, and a very long cart
transporting an enormous slab of Sienna marble.

"Would you mind terribly if we didn't go to the
museum today?" she asked.

He turned to her, a puzzled look on his face.
"But I thought it was *you* who wanted to see it."

"Oh, I do very much.

"Then?"

Her pale brown eyebrows lowered, she looked
deep in contemplation. She exhaled. "You said we
were to share everything."

"Yes."

"I think my uncle may have been murdered."

Murder was such a vile thing. He'd never
personally known a person who had been
murdered, never even thought of such a thing
touching him personally. It had never crossed his
mind that Simon Hastings could have been
murdered, but now that she had put voice to it, he
realized her suspicion had merit.

Those who knew Hastings kept commenting on
how the man had been in his prime. And five-and-
fifty wasn't *that* old. No one had heard of Hastings
having been sick. One didn't just suddenly
become ill and die immediately. Even those
gravely ill, in his experience, lingered for a good
while before dying.

How in the blazes was it that his wife, so young and so innocent in the ways of the world, could have possibly come to such a realization? He slowly turned to her, once more seeing her with new eyes. He no longer thought of her as a lost puppy dog. She was most definitely a woman. A very lovely woman now that her French maid was arranging her hair so elegantly. And she was clever, far more clever than he'd originally thought. "Why do you say that?"

"I believe Uncle Simon was poisoned, and I believe the person who changed the will is the one responsible for his death."

"What makes you believe he was poisoned?"

"Several things. First, the fact that he'd not been sick. The fact he . . . vomited. I've read about persons who are poisoned. They always lose the contents of their stomach before keeling over, dead."

He nodded. "That's true. Any other reason?"

"Yes, actually. That day when you found the name of Uncle's solicitor in his library, I was poking about the room, looking for things that would tell me about my uncle. I never for a moment imagined he'd been murdered. I thought at the time it was perfectly natural that one of his age could just die, but I was being immature. I now realize that he must have been in good physical condition."

"I agree, from what I've been told."

"In his library I was able, I think, to ascertain the chair where my uncle always sat. The cushion on it was worn almost flat. The table beside it had rings from glasses that had been set there over the years, but no glass sat there.

"However, there was a glass at the chair

opposite, the one a guest would have sat in. I believe that's where the murderer, having come as a friend, sat. I believe he somehow put poison in Uncle's glass, watched him die, then cleaned up the poison glass before leaving."

"And the murderer made sure to come on a night when all the servants were off."

"That was vital for his success. He made the single mistake of forgetting to remove his own glass. Were it not for that glass—so far away from Uncle's chair that I knew it couldn't be his—I never would have known there was a visitor, never would have grown suspicious."

"So what is our next step?" He shocked himself. He was deferring to his youthful bride.

"First, I should like to speak to his housekeeper."

"Then we'll go back home, and I'll get her address from where I put it in my library."

"No need. I remember. Mrs. Thornton. She's now employed at 151 Camden Street."

"Ah, beauty and brains. How fortunate am I."

She blushed. He'd never been with a woman who blushed. Certainly Maria, with her dark skin, did not blush. But then he realized a woman of Maria's ilk would not likely blush, even if she had been as fair as Emma.

$\mathcal{C}$hapter 11

Mrs. Thornton had come down in the world. The street where the late Simon Hastings lived in the heart of Mayfair was one of the most fashionable in London. Camden Street was a proper upper middle-class neighborhood. It was the kind of place where Emmott or Wycliff would live. Perhaps a physician. More typically, men who earned their living would live here. As opposed to Mayfair where the majority of the landowners were aristocrats or those with very hefty purses.

Anyone here in Camden Town would leap at the prospect of hiring a housekeeper who'd recently been engaged in Mayfair.

Well aware of his own cultured voice, Adam told the butler at 151 Camden Street they needed a few moments of Mrs. Thornton's time regarding her last employer. Eyeing how well dressed Emma was (and Adam thought she looked exceptionally pretty), the butler asked that they step into the morning room.

They passed through a dark corridor that featured a narrow wooden staircase and came to the neatly kept morning room where the opened draperies allowed sun into the chamber. Adam and his wife sat next to each other on a dark green settee that was perfectly serviceable but modest and bit dreary.

A few moments later a neatly dressed middle-aged woman came into the chamber.

Adam stood and introduced himself. "You are Mrs. Thornton?" he asked.

"I am." Mrs. Thornton looked at Emma.

"I," Emma said, "am Simon Hastings' niece, and I should like to ask you some questions about him. Please sit."

The housekeeper sat on a wooden arm chair facing Emma. Her face went somber as she offered Emma condolences. "Your uncle was greatly looking forward to you coming. He authorized me to completely refurnish our prettiest bedchamber for you." She sighed. "I wish you could have seen it."

"I do, too," Emma said solemnly. "How I wish I could have seen my uncle, gotten to know him. I feel so cheated."

"He said you were an orphan, and he was responsible for you."

Emma's eyes misted. "I haven't come here to talk about me. I need to know about my uncle, need to know about his . . . death. I understand my uncle spent a good deal of time in his library."

"Indeed he did, miss. He loved to read by the fire. Always in his same shabby chair. Even though he was a wealthy man, he loved that chair!"

Emma cracked a smile. "Did he, by chance, give orders that his library not be cleaned regularly?"

Mrs. Thornton folded her hands in her lap. "I wonder how you should know that! He did not want the parlor maid disturbing his books at all. The library was the only room that wasn't cleaned daily. Though cleaning was not included in my duties, I personally cleaned Mr. Hastings' library on the first day of each month. I was the only one he trusted. He kept private papers in his desk there."

"How long did you serve my uncle?

Now, Mrs. Thornton's eyes misted. "Since the day he moved into his house five-and-twenty years ago."

"I am sorry for *your* loss," Emma said to her. "You and my uncle must have gotten on very well, and you must have been pleased to make your home on Curzon Street with him."

"He was the kindest man. No one could ever have a finer employer. I miss him dreadfully. He did leave me a nice legacy. I plan to tuck away my earnings here on Camden Street for ten years. They should be enough to buy me a little cottage somewhere in the country. I'll have a garden for my food, and your uncle's pension to tide me over year in, year out for the rest of my life. I owe much to him."

Adam wanted to change the topic before both women got too weepy. "We have received a list of Mr. Hastings' servants," Adam said. "It appears it was a fairly small staff. A valet. One cook. Two parlor maids. A butler and housekeeper."

"Mr. Hastings lived alone. He never entertained and rarely had visitors. His eating tastes were simple, hence a single scullery worker," Mrs. Thornton said.

"Do you know men named Jonathan Booker or Sidney Wolf?" he asked.

She shook her head.

Adam blew out a breath. "Was it Mr. Hastings' custom to give all the servants the entire day and night off every Sunday?"

Mrs. Thornton nodded. "From the day he

bought the house. He once told me he looked forward to being completely alone one day a week." She paused, her eyes downcast. "The butler said Mr. Hastings told him he liked to walk about the house without his clothes. I believed Mr. Hastings was just jesting."

Adam chuckled.

"You mean his servants were not even allowed to stay in their own rooms on Sundays?" Emma asked.

"Only if they were sick. He encouraged us to go to Sunday service. Then we could do whatever we wished—walk about in the park or visit friends or family. "

"What hours were the servants gone on Sunday?" Adam asked.

"We usually left by nine in the morning and returned anywhere between nine at night and midnight."

"Did my uncle say he was expecting a visitor the night he died?"

Mrs. Thornton shook her head. "Your uncle normally did not have visitors. He said he dealt with many people at the tea company all day, that he enjoyed a quiet home. He only used three chambers: the library, his bedchamber, and the dinner room."

"Had my uncle been sick before his death? Had he missed going to the tea company?"

The housekeeper shook her head. "He had not been sick at all."

"Finding his body," Adam said in a grave voice, "must have been a harrowing experience, and I'm very sorry you had to be the one, Mrs. Thornton. I'm even more sorry that I have to ask you some questions about that morning."

She shut her eyes tightly. "It was horrible. I shall never be able to efface that vision from my mind." She shook her head and peered at Emma. "It's very hard to lose someone you care for, but to see them like that- - -" She burst into tears.

Adam wondered if he could have handled that better.

Emma leapt to her feet and went to comfort the weeping woman, whilst glaring at him. "I'm so sorry, Mrs. Thornton." Emma cupped a hand on the woman's arm. "I am so grateful that Uncle had you to care for him."

Mrs. Thornton looked up at Emma through bleary eyes and attempted a smile.

"I know it's difficult," Adam said, "but can you describe the scene when you found him?"

The housekeeper nodded, sniffing. She began, but her voice was thin, like that of one just short of hysteria. Made him feel like a bloody reprobate.

"Davis—that's Mr. Hastings' valet—told me Mr. Hastings hadn't slept in his bed. On a few occasions Mr. Hastings fell asleep in the library, so I went there with the intention of awakening him. It wasn't like him to sleep so late." She stopped and drew a shaky breath. "When I walked into the library, he was sitting in his chair. At first I thought he was asleep, but as I came closer, I saw the . . . the vomit down the front of him." Here her voice was a low moan. "Thinking he was sick, I stood there asking him in a loud voice if there was anything I could do for him. There was nooooooo answer," she wailed.

After a short pause, she continued. "It was a moment before the idea that he might be dead slammed into me. I froze. I couldn't bring myself to determine if he was still alive. I turned around and raced up the stairs to get Davis.

"Davis is the one who felt for a pulse. His face was ashen and he was trembling mightily when he turned around and told me Mr. Hastings was dead. It was such a shock to both of us because Mr. Hastings had always been so healthy. Cook blamed herself. Said he'd never have had a stomach complaint if he'd eaten her food. She had left him some of Saturday's bread and some cheeses, but she thinks he must have eaten elsewhere, and it must have killed him."

"What happened next?" Adam asked.

"Davis said he would clean up his master. He and the butler carried Mr. Hastings upstairs, and laid him on his bed. I asked the downstairs parlor maid to clean around Mr. Hastings's chair. Then I got out of the room and never went back. It was too painful. "

"Did Uncle die in his favorite chair?" Emma asked.

Mrs. Thornton nodded.

"Was there a glass beside his chair? Perhaps an empty glass?"

"There was no glass. I looked at his table to see if there was something there that could have made him so sick."

* * *

Once they were back in the carriage, Emma turned to him. "I feel so flat. I feel as if my suspicions have been validated, but there's no joy in knowing my poor uncle was most likely murdered."

He covered her hand with his. "There can't possibly be joy in such knowledge, but I am most proud of my wife for her fine deductive reasoning."

His comment lifted the mantle of gloom which

had settled on her. "What do you think we should do next, my dearest husband?" How she loved saying that! How she wished she could use true endearments with him. He only used his endearments to convince others theirs was a normal marriage.

"I'm thinking we shall need Sawyer's lock-picking talents once again."

"You mean to go back inside Uncle's house again?"

He squeezed her hand. "Unless it would be too painful for you."

"It will be painful, since I feel as if I know him a little better after getting Mrs. Thornton's perspective, but I'm angry, too. I don't care about the money or the house or the tea company. I care that my kindly uncle was cruelly murdered—and for no other reason than to steal his fortune. I'll not stop until the thieving, murdering spawn of Lucifer is brought to justice." She glared at him. "I, sir, happen to believe there's a devil."

"If there is, then the man who killed your uncle deserves his fiery fate. Your uncle sounded like an admirable man. I'm sorry I wasn't a more friendly neighbor."

"Don't be. Had he wanted more friends, he would have made overtures. From what Mrs. Thornton said, his chief interest and the thing that pleased him most was sitting in his library. Just him and his books."

"I still wish I'd known him."

"So do I," she said solemnly.

"I'm trying to decide if we've enough time to do a thorough search of his house today, or if we should wait until tomorrow and devote the entire day to it." He put his arm around her shoulders and drew her closer. "Don't forget we go to the theatre tonight, and I want you to be ravishing."

Her bows lowered. "I'm not quite sure how the word ravishing applies to a woman in a theatre box."

He chuckled. "You don't need to know, my dear one. It was not the best choice of words. I should have said I want all eyes in the theatre on my beautiful wife tonight. Will it take you long to prepare?"

"Actually, it will. Perhaps it's best we do go back to Uncle's tomorrow."

* * *

He had told her that Therese was not to put the amethyst necklace on her. "I want that pleasure myself. Once you're dressed, have your maid tap at my door."

Now Emma sat before her looking glass, hardly recognizing the woman in its reflection as herself. She was completely dressed in her new lavender gown and thought nothing could ever be lovelier than her dress.

But it was Therese's artistry with hair that made Emma look as if she were a leader of fashion—in the highest circles. Not only was her hair swept back beautifully, but Therese had pinned diamonds throughout. A duchess's coronet could not have been lovelier. Her heart filled to capacity when she thought of Adam's kindness in procuring the diamond pins and giving them to Therese for his wife's hair. He knew so much more about what was fashionable than Emma.

Her stomach coiled as she sat waiting for Therese to return from knocking on Adam's door. Would he think her pretty?

Her heart stampeded when he strolled into her

bedchamber, the velvet jewel box in his hand.

He stopped just past the doorway and stared. "My god, you're lovely!"

She finally exhaled and timidly said, "Thank you."

He came to her and placed the Bourbon jewels around her neck. She watched in the looking glass and was mesmerized, so awed over how beautiful the necklace was she did not even see Adam's handsome reflection.

When he finished, he commanded her to stand. "I want to see the full effect."

She did as bid, once more holding her breath. She was a bit embarrassed over the low cut in the front of her gown. It barely covered her small bosom, yet somehow made her breasts seem larger than they really were.

Aunt Harriett would have been mortified. She would never have allowed Emma out of her bedchamber in so scandalous a dress.

Emma blushed as her husband stood back and lazily perused her from the tip of her head to the slippers on her feet. His gaze missed nothing.

Without saying a word, he came forward and planted a kiss on top her head. "I shall be the most envied man at the theatre tonight. You are perfection." Then he offered his arm, and they left for Drury Lane.

She felt as if she were a celestial being, her heart and her step were so light. *He thinks I am perfection.* He kissed her on the top of her head.

Once they were in the Birmingham box at the theatre, they were soon joined by William and Lady Sophia. "Emma," Lady Sophia exclaimed, "you look as if you could be a Russian princess or something equally grand. And, of course, you are utterly beautiful."

"I owe much to Therese. I'm so grateful you sent her to me. I could not be happier."

"I knew she would be perfect, but she did only your hair—and she did that beautifully—but you cannot credit her for your supreme loveliness."

"You're too kind."

Their conversation was cut short as the candles were snuffed, and the curtain went up. As fascinated as Emma was to see a Shakespearian play in person, she was too exhilarated by *everything* to follow the actors' words as closely as she should. She spent more time looking at the audience, taking in all the beautiful gowns, each one varied from the others.

She was in awe of the baroque u-shaped theatre with its high walls ringed with luxurious boxes. They looked like gilded pockets. Many of them were filled with the nobility, some of whom she recognized from the illustrations in the periodicals Auntie received. There was Lady Waverly in turquoise across the way, and Emma was quite sure the Duke and Duchess of Gorham were in one of the boxes that faced the stage.

She drew in her breath when she realized the notorious courtesan Mary Steele (caricatured so often in the press that Emma had come to recognize her) sat on one of the lower- rung boxes. Emma must have stared at her for ten minutes. She'd never thought she would ever see so scandalous a woman in the flesh. Whatever she had expected to see was not this. The woman appeared perfectly normal. Were she passing Emma on the street, Emma would not take notice of the rather plain woman.

Had she thought perhaps Mrs. Steele would be

sprouting horns like some Beelzebub? Or be dressed so indecently that parts that shouldn't show, did so?

Emma felt less guilty for not watching the play when she realized most of those who sat in the boxes were also gawking at those in the other boxes.

Was it her imagination, or were many of them training their eyes—and their opera glasses—on the Birmingham box? Most likely because the Birmingham brothers were so handsome. Then she was reminded of her husband's words about being the envy of every man there. Those people couldn't be looking at her.

Could they?

Even though Adam had said she was lovely and that she was perfection, and Lady Sophia had said she was beautiful, and even though her looking glass displayed an uncommonly pretty woman, Emma refused to believe any of those people could be interested in a nothing like her.

Before Emma had the good fortune to wed Adam, she would have been thrilled just to be able to stand on the floor below with the rest of the masses. Even now, she still expected to be told there had been a ghastly mistake, and that she must go back to Upper Barrington.

After the third act of *Richard III*, which was much too grim for her taste, the sconces around the theatre's perimeter were lighted. She turned to her husband. "But it's not over!"

He chuckled and drew her close. "I forget you have no theatres in Upper Baddington. This is intermission. People will go visit other boxes or procure refreshments during this break before the final two acts."

She gave him a mock glare. "Barrington."

He laughed again, then stood. "Excuse me whilst I go for refreshments."

* * *

Adam felt as if he were a member of the Royal Family when he descended the stairs and was mobbed by half the men he knew from White's. All of them wanted to know who was the—and they *did* use the word *ravishing*—woman he'd brought. He felt as if he'd grown a foot taller.

"Sirs, I beg you not use the word *ravishing* in connection with my wife."

They gasped.

"We did not know you'd wed," Lord Tremayne said.

William came to his side. "Gentlemen, my brother is newly married."

"You Birminghams all have an eye for everything exquisite," Lord Ruggles said.

Adam turned to the earl and bowed. "I thank you, my lord. I count myself most fortunate. Now, if you'll excuse me, I must procure refreshments for my wife."

After the play, it was some ten minutes before his carriage was brought along, owing to the large number of theatre-goers awaiting their own conveyances. Once in their coach, Emma said, "How fortunate we were that we didn't have to wait an hour. Look at all the fine lords and ladies who are still waiting!"

He dared not tell her he paid handsomely for his driver to be one of the earliest in the queue.

"I was correct when I predicted I'd be the most envied man in the theatre tonight."

Her eyes widened. "You can't mean the people actually noticed me?"

"I most certainly can. They did. I was almost accosted by men clamoring to know who was the beautiful woman at my side tonight."

Her lashes lowered. "You're just saying that to flatter me."

He lifted her chin and eyed her. "I'm saying it because it's the truth. And you were the loveliest woman there tonight."

She started to protest that Lady Sophia was far lovelier—which was the truth—but for once, for the first time in her entire life, she wanted to bask in the warmth of his praise. No one had ever in her life told her she was pretty. For this night, sitting here beside the man who owned her heart, she wanted to be lovely. "Thank you," she whispered.

"So, dear one, was this you first play?"

She was powerless to control her wide smile. "It was, and it's been the most exciting night of my entire life."

He laughed. "Has it occurred to you that each successive day has been *the most exciting ever*? How nice it must be to see the world in hyperbole."

"Oh, but it's the truth." She shrugged. "I know it may sound as if I speak in hyperbole."

"There's nothing wrong with having so positive an outlook," he said, smiling. "I'm happy to hear that you enjoyed tonight. I want London to be exciting for you."

"I've never had excitement in my life, and now I'm rather embroiled in it."

"Right down to a murder"

"In a way, it is rather exciting. I daresay I would never have had the opportunity to investigate a murder in Upper Barrington."

He chuckled.

* * *

Once they reached the Curzon Street house, he walked her to her bedchamber. He felt as if he were in some rose-scented stupor of blossoming affection for this enticing little package of femininity he had made his wife. "Good night, dear one." He lowered his head and settled a light kiss upon her lips. "You are beautiful."

As he pulled back, her eyes widened. Good lord, had he scared her?

What had gotten into him? He'd not thought about kissing her. It had just happened as naturally as one reaches to pet a dog.

"Good night," she returned, no malice in her sweet voice.

Long after he'd undressed, long after the candles had been snuffed, he still remembered her wide-eyed look when he'd shocked her with his unwanted kiss. His own thoughtlessness rankled him.

He vowed to better control himself in the future.

$\mathcal{C}$hapter 12

"Madame, what has happened to make you look so happy?" Therese asked when Emma floated into the chamber, a dreamy smile upon her face.

Emma lowered herself before the dressing table. She could not very well tell her maid she was happy because her husband had just kissed her. She wanted the servants to believe theirs was a normal marriage. "This was the most wonderful night I've ever spent."

"And I believe madame was greatly admired, no?" Therese began to remove the diamond pins from Emma's hair.

Emma shyly nodded. "I hate to take off my dress. I've felt like a . . . princess all night."

"You look like a princess." Therese began to brush out her mistress's hair. "Ah, but you have so many other lovely gowns your must look forward to wearing. You will be more beautiful than all of them."

When Therese finished brushing her hair, Emma stood and allowed her maid to assist her in undressing, then dressing for bed.

After Therese left, carefully carrying away the lavender gown, Emma climbed atop her bed, still smiling and still whirling from the night's exhilaration. But most of all from Adam's kiss. It had been the most pleasurable thing she'd ever experienced—hyperbole notwithstanding. She'd been completely unprepared for Adam's kiss and, therefore, shocked. She prayed her stiff reaction hadn't repulsed him for she very much wanted to be given another chance to kiss him.

The notion of him kissing her *had* to demonstrate his growing affection for her, did it not? It had certainly been the perfect climax to a perfect night. (She really did speak and think in hyperbole. Would that it would always be warranted.)

She wished she knew him better, knew better how to gauge him. It had been impossible for her to understand his reaction to their kiss. She thought perhaps—even though he was hard to read— he might have regretted it. On the other hand, right after the kiss, he *had* told her she was beautiful.

She should have responded more favorably, should have been a better participant. She was so woefully inexperienced she didn't know what one did during a kiss. One thing she knew for certain: she wanted him to kiss her again. Hopefully, next time her response would be more to his liking.

* * *

"Where are you going?" her husband asked the following morning as Emma began to climb her uncle's stairs to the upper floors.

She turned around and met his gaze, a solemn look on her face. "I wanted to see what was supposed to have been my chamber."

His demeanor softened. "I'll come with you."

Her eyes brightened, and her mouth lifted into a grin. "You're afraid I'll turn into a watering pot."

"I most sincerely hope you do not." He came

and offered his arm for support. "I suppose we should also look at your uncle's bedchamber. We might find something helpful there."

"Seeing his chamber will make me sad."

He covered her hand with his and nodded grimly.

"Leave that to me."

"No. I need to go."

On the second floor, he opened the first door. "This must be your uncle's bedchamber." He strode across the dark room and drew open the draperies.

Uncle Simon's bedchamber was austere for a man wealthy enough to live on Curzon Street. There were no fine fabrics or hand-painted papers on the walls, which were painted in a royal blue that matched his bed coverings. From beneath a gold cornice hung draperies of the same blue with a gold diamond pattern.

The chimneypiece of fine cream-coloured marble held a wooden case clock resting on four gilded feet. It was the room's only ornament.

Obviously her uncle used this chamber only for its intended purpose. She was surprised there was no writing desk. That must mean he did all of his writing in the library.

"I doubt there are any clues here," Adam said.

She shook her head sadly. "Nothing to reveal anything about him as a man."

He came to settle an arm about her. "His last letter to you revealed what manner of man he was. Noble."

Adam's words were comforting.

The room next to Uncle Simon's was to have been hers. She drew open the draperies, and the pale yellow chamber was bathed in light. That the gilded, high tester bed looked as if it had recently been purchased touched her deeply. Had she never seen Adam's house, she would have thought this the loveliest bed imaginable. The walls of canary yellow were recently painted. If she inhaled deeply, she could still smell the paint.

As she examined the bedcovering of yellow silk, she realized it was not only new, but also of fine quality. No imitation silk. Mrs. Thornton would only have procured such lovely things if her employer had authorized it. How generous her dear uncle had been.

She turned and went for the door. "I've seen enough," she said in a trembling voice.

Once in her uncle's dark library, she first drew open the drapes to allow good light, then she showed her husband her uncle's favorite chair. "See how worn down the cushion is?"

He nodded. "I understand what Mrs. Thornton was talking about. It looks as if that chair was the place where he was most comfortable."

"And over here is the glass . . ." Her mouth gaped open. "It's gone!"

"What's gone?"

"The murderer's glass!"

His brows lowered. "Perhaps you just *thought* you saw a glass there. No one else could have gained access to this house."

Anger bolted through her. "I'm positive there was a glass next to the visitor's chair." A prickly chill inched up her spine. Her terrified gaze circled the library. "He's been here."

Adam's gaze darkened. "Sawyer did say it looked to him that someone had been whittling at the door since the last time he tampered with it."

She collapsed onto her uncle's chair, clutching

her chest. "Dear God. This is frightening." The only thing saving her from being paralyzed with fear was her husband's presence. Her determined gaze took in his towering strength from his booted feet planted so close to her, along his long, muscled legs sheathed in fine buckskin to his broad-shouldered torso. He looked more powerful than the most decorated military hero. Even though he wore no sword, she felt exempt from danger as long as she was with him. *My husband.* Instinctively she knew he would always protect her. Since that first night, he had looked after her.

"Forgive me," he said. "I know you saw a glass next to the visitor's seat the last time we were here."

"He must have remembered and sneaked back in here to remove it—and any sign that my uncle might have had a visitor that last night."

"I wonder if there was anything else he thought might incriminate him."

"I suppose there could have been a note or letter from the murderer to inform Uncle Simon he would be calling on him that Sunday evening."

He leveled a grave look at her. "You might as well say his name, Emma. There's little doubt James Ashburnham's the murderer."

She shivered. "It's mortifying to think we've been in the same room with such an evil person. You even spoke to him."

He nodded grimly. "I suggest we stop talking about murder and try to look for something that might help us prove Ashburnham's guilt."

They both moved to stand in front of her uncle's desk. "Since you looked at the top last time, I will now," she said.

"I'll start with the drawers on the right."

"Wait!" She snatched a single sheet of paper. "Look at this! It was right on top of Uncle Simon's ledger."

They both read. *I should like to call on you Sunday evening on a personal matter. —Faukes*

"Was this note here the last time we were in the library?"

He shook his head. "Absolutely not."

"Then Ashburnham forged it to point the guilt at my uncle's business partner." What a diabolical plan.

"Who better to forge the handwriting of both his employers than a man who serves as their clerk?" He took the note and placed it in his pocket.

She shook her head gravely. "How could someone betray those he worked so closely with?"

"We will never understand the mind of a murderer."

"It's so upsetting to know that fiend has been here."

He nodded. "Had I known, I would have had the house guarded."

"Even if we caught him in the act, it wouldn't have proven anything."

"True. We need real evidence." He opened the drawer he'd been about to inspect.

With a sigh, she scanned the top of her uncle's desk. A tall, cloth-bound ledger was the largest thing on it. She began to examine its pages. Her uncle kept detailed records of household expenses, accounting for every farthing, down to the quarterly expenditure for candles. Her brows hiked. She'd never realized how costly it was to light a house this size. Oddly fascinated by the ledger, she sank into the desk chair to peruse it. There were payments for the green grocer, the coal, the *Morning Chronicle*, a tithe to his church, and small sums she would never have thought to calculate. She went through a dozen pages. Seeing his neat numerals and getting a glimpse into his exacting nature, she felt closer to him but bitter that she would never know him in the flesh.

Since it was of no use to her present inquiry, she reluctantly closed the book. The surface of his desk was untidy. It appeared her uncle had difficulty getting rid of communication, whether they be tradesmen's bills or two-month-old newspapers. These varied papers were not neatly stacked. Had her uncle left it this way, or had the mur- -, James Ashburnham messed it whilst looking for something?

Thinking of Ashburnham going through her uncle's personal papers made her furious. She almost laughed at herself. Examining her uncle's papers was not even a fraction as evil as premeditated murder. She prayed her uncle's murder would be avenged.

"Was this desk as messy the day you found out Mr. Wycliff's address?" she asked.

Adam stopped rummaging through the second drawer and eyed the desk. "It was by no means tidy, but it does look as if someone else has been here."

That prickly chill returned, creeping down her spine. Confirmation was not comforting.

She drew a deep breath and returned to the task. Ideally, she sought a slip of paper from Ashburnham, begging to meet with Uncle Simon Sunday. A solitary man like her uncle had little in the way of personal correspondence.

"Look at this," Adam said, handing her a stack of letters tied together with string. "Your uncle appears to have kept every letter you sent."

"Let me see." With a lump in her throat, she thumbed through the letters. Those on the bottom had been written when she was a little girl. How touched she was that he'd kept each of them.

With misty eyes, she looked up and met Adam's solemn gaze. "I beg you not to turn into a watering pot," he said.

Despite her sadness, she laughed.

"You know, pet, I don't think we're going to find anything—now that we know Ashburnham's been here. Anything that would have established his presence here Sunday has been destroyed."

"I know you're right, but I hate to give up."

He cupped his hand on her shoulder. "We're not giving up. I swear to you."

Their eyes locked. In that instant she knew he had absorbed all her troubles as his own. She was almost overwhelmed. Adam was the only person she had ever been this close to. Powerless to stop herself, she placed a hand on his forearm.

"We go into the City next. My tea shipment has arrived," he said.

"So we shall have our own example of James Ashburnham's handwriting."

* * *

"I doubt if a lady has ever stepped inside this building," Adam told her as his coach came to a stop in front of Number 23 Cheapstowe. Being on a questionable street in the East End, this was not a place where any of the Birminghams conducted business. The building was more of a storage facility for their construction projects.

He looked at the building with fresh eyes and realized it could use a bit of refurbishing. The red bricks had to be a hundred years old, and the structure leaned to the right. A new coat of paint was also needed around the eaves. He'd bring up the matter with William, who—now that he was married—served as a domestic problem solver for all the Birmingham interests. Lady Sophia had put her foot down, forbidding her husband to conduct clandestine activities that could land him in prison—or in a grave.

Old Riley let them into the ill-lit warehouse. "That shipment what came late yesterday be right over here, sir."

Fortunately, it was far beneath a clerestory window which shone directly on the stack of boxes. Adam asked Riley for a knife. He then neatly excised the address square from the box on top. "That's all I need for now. Help yourself and the missus to a box of tea."

Riley's eyes widened. "A box that size will last the rest of our lives!"

Adam chuckled as he walked away and proffered his arm to his wife. "We return to Mr. Emmott's now. Perhaps he's gotten an opinion from his handwriting expert."

"And now you'll need the expert to look at this."

He patted his pocket. "That and the note alleged to have been written by Harold Faukes."

"Should you not have something written in Mr. Faukes' hand to compare it to?"

"An excellent suggestion, dear one. We will first go to the Ceylon Tea Company."

She gasped. "I don't know if I can stand to be near that horrible murderer."

"I know, love. But he doesn't know that we know." He pressed her hand. "You have no reason to worry when I'm with you. I will always protect you."

"I know," she whispered.

$\mathcal{C}$hapter 13

She had been so terrified at the prospect of coming face to face with James Ashburnham that when the carriage came to a stop in front of the Ceylon Tea Company Emma could not bring herself to leave the coach.

Adam turned to her, took both her hands, and spoke in a gentle voice. "I vow I would lay down my life before I'd ever let anyone harm you."

What woman could be unaffected by such a proclamation? She nodded, and he helped her from their coach. Having Adam by her side as she entered the tea company made her feel invincible—but still upset about having to be so close to her uncle's killer.

"I know you're nervous," he said, "but force yourself to act normal. Ignore him if you'd like, but don't be transparent."

Upstairs, he faced Ashburnham and spoke with confidence of one born to command. "Adam Birmingham to see Mr. Faukes." (She was so proud of her husband.)

Nodding, the clerk left his desk and went into his employer's office, this time leaving the door open. Seconds later, he exited as his employer came to the door to issue a greeting. "Do come in, Mr. and Mrs. Birmingham."

Adam was sure to close the door before he sat

at the sofa.

"What can I do for you today?"

Adam produced the note. "Did you send this to Mr. Hastings?" he asked in a lowered voice.

Faukes' eyes squinted, then he took a pair of spectacles from his pocket and read the letter, his brows drawn together as he frowned. "I never saw it before, never sent it—even if it does look like my handwriting."

Adam pressed his index finger to his lips, tossing a gaze toward the door.

Faukes nodded, then lowered his voice. "Not only did I not write it, I've never been in Simon's house. There was no need. We saw each other every day, six days a week."

He examined the letter once more, shaking his head. "How in the devil could someone have copied my handwriting so accurately? Unless . . ." His gaze darted to the door to the outer chamber, but he clamped shut his mouth and did not continue.

"Does Mr. Ashburnham sometimes sign your name for you when you're busy—or out of the office?" Adam asked.

"As a matter of fact, he does."

"Was it his custom to also forge Mr. Hastings' signature?"

Faukes nodded. "We both trusted him. He's been employed here for ten years. Never has a penny gone missing."

"I understand. It's imperative that one has employees who can be trusted."

"Dear God!" Faukes exclaimed. "Was this Sunday the night Simon died?"

Adam and Emma both gravely nodded.

Faukes' face blanched. "Was Simon murdered?"

Adam once more pressed his index finger to his mouth and spoke in a hoarse whisper. "We believe he might have been."

"And the murderer's trying to plant evidence to implicate me?"

"We believe that may be the case," Adam responded.

"It wasn't me," Mr. Faukes said. "Simon was my friend."

"We didn't think it was you," Emma reassured him.

A vicious look surged across Mr. Faukes' face. "That vile clerk! I can't even send him packing since he's now half owner!" He peered at Emma and spoke pleadingly. "You must challenge the will. "

"We have," she said.

Faukes closed his eyes as if he were in pain. "How am I to work with him when I know he's a murderer, know that he's murdered my closest friend?"

Adam continued speaking in a low voice. "You must pretend you know nothing, that you suspect nothing."

A pained expression on his face, Faukes nodded. "Is there anything I can do to help with this nasty business?"

"Can you tell me if Ashburnham's the only person in the company who addresses the shipping labels?" Adam asked.

"Yes, he's the only one."

Adam stood. "We're going to see if we can conduct a search of my wife's uncle's office now."

"Your timing couldn't be better. Ashburnham's planning to move into Simon's office tomorrow."

"I suspect he's already destroyed anything that

might point to his guilt," Emma whispered, "but we're going to have a look."

Faukes wrote his home address on a piece of paper and handed it to Emma. "If you ever need to see me in private."

When they left his office, Adam explained to Ashburnham, "My wife would like to recover her letters and any other personal objects from her uncle's office, if you have no objections, Mr. Ashburnham."

"Be my guest," he said. What his voice lacked in malice, his glare made up for.

A cold shiver snaked down Emma's spine as she swiftly moved away from the man's chilling presence.

Her uncle's office was considerably tidier than his library. All of his papers were confined to the large desk which was placed close to the tall casement. "Shall I do the top while you start on the drawers?" she asked.

"We're acting like a long-married couple, practically reading each others' minds."

Smiling, she flicked a glance at him. Their eyes held. There was such warmth in his gaze she could not look away for a moment. Her husband had the power to suffuse her with a warmth that destroyed Ashburnham's iciness.

She thumbed through a stack of shipping leaflets on Uncle's desk. They were tables of shipping dates and times, each from a different sailing company. Another stack contained invoices from various tradesmen ranging from a tin company in Cornwall to a paper supplier in London.

On the opposite desk corner was a stack of letters to various grocers, inns, and hoteliers in an attempt to procure orders for the Ceylon Tea Company, each letter awaiting Hastings' signature. One fine leather-bound book contained addresses for all her uncle's associates. All the entries were in her uncle's unmistakable hand. She was pleased yet saddened to see her Upper Barrington address there.

It saddened her, too, to recognize his sealing stamp right next to the crimson wax.

When she finished, she turned to her husband. "Nothing here. Need help?"

Busy reading a small book—much smaller than his hands—he ignored her.

"What's that?"

His lashes lifted, and he put index finger to mouth. "It's an occurrence book."

"And for last Sunday?"

Their gazes locked. "The page has been torn out."

Her heartbeat roared. She felt violated. "We must get out of here at once." If she didn't, she was afraid she'd be sick.

* * *

Adam had never seen her like this before. He lowered the blind on his carriage window and pulled her close. She was trembling violently. "It's all right."

"I can n-n-never go back there again."

"I promise I won't make you." He lifted her chin. "What did I tell you earlier, Emma?"

"You vowed that you'd never let anyone harm me."

He closed his other arm around her, completely enveloping her in his embrace. He wanted to make her feel safe. Though his actions were motivated by his desire to protect her, he felt a cheater. For it was he who was profoundly moved by the feel of her slight body within the circle of his arms. This was not a helpless girl he held. She was a woman.

A desirable woman.

For his own tranquility of thought, he was glad that the drive to Emmott's office was but a short distance. When the coach stopped, he loosened his hold on her. "Nothing to fear at Mr. Emmott's, dear one."

It suddenly occurred to him Emma had become very dear to him. Not in the same way as Maria. Entirely different.

In Emmott's office, they received welcome news. "My penmanship expert will testify that the will is a forgery. Even though it was a very good forgery, especially the deceased's signature, he says he can point out that the *descenders*, those letters which go below the line of writing, are fundamentally different than Mr. Hastings'. He said it would have been impossible for Mr. Hastings to have drafted that later will."

"But did you not say that kind of testimony may not hold up in court?" she asked.

"I have a plan. I will gather testimonials from a half a dozen respected leaders that point to our expert's credibility. "

"That sounds interesting, but you've got to have more than that," Adam said.

Emmott eyed him. "Have you come up with anything?"

Adam shrugged. "Not really." He pulled the forged Faukes' letter from his pocket, along with some authentic examples of Faukes' handwriting and handed them to his solicitor. "This is what we believe to be a forged letter. Mr. Faukes swears he did not write it. Here are examples of his penmanship." Adam explained the background.

"I'll have my expert examine these, too."

"And," Adam added, producing the shipping label from the Ceylon Tea Company, "this bears the handwriting of the suspected forger. See if your expert can see a link between his penmanship and the forged will."

* * *

"Where do we go next?" she asked.

"I'm going to drop you at Lady Fiona's. She wants to educate you all about Almack's. We go there tonight. I will have the opportunity to display my lovely wife."

Her heartbeat thundered. She was exhilarated at the same time she was nervous. Adam expected her to be greatly admired in her lavender dress and the Bourbon jewels, but she knew next to the beautiful Ladies Fiona and Sophia she would look like a mouse—even in her stunning amethyst and diamond necklace.

In spite of her misgivings, she was thrilled to be going to the famed Almack's she had read so much about. Only those in the highest echelons of Society received the coveted vouchers for the once-weekly ball. She would have been thrilled even to have been one of the punch servers in order to gape at the *beau monde*.

"And what will you be doing this afternoon?" she asked him.

"I shall put in a long-overdue appearance at my bank."

"I'm sorry you've neglected your duties because of me."

He took her hand and kissed it. "Don't be. I've enjoyed every moment."

* * *

How, she wondered that night, had the insipid assemblies she'd attended previously prepared her for the pinnacle of assemblies—that at the august chambers of Almack's? If she were a wagering person, she would bet that every lady here had been taught by a dancing master. Since there were no dancing masters in either Upper Barrington or Lower Barrington, her cousin Annabelle, who was Sir Arthur's granddaughter and who had made her debut into London Society, had given Emma enough instructions that she cut a very dashing figure at the assemblies in Nottingham, the closest town of any size to the Barringtons.

Would those here know she was but an imposter? Even if she did don a necklace which had come from one of the great European royal families. Dear, dear Adam knew how insecure she felt and had promised he would partner her for the first country dance as well as the first waltz.

Upon entering the brightly lit ballroom, Lady Sophia presented her to Ladies Cowper and Jersey. Emma's heart pounded so furiously she was afraid the stalwarts of London Society would hear it. Ever since she could remember she had read about Almack's and the aristocratic patronesses who screened each applicant as strictly as a father grills his daughter's suitors. To her astonishment, the patronesses welcomed her with bright smiles and compliments on her beautiful necklace. She never would have boasted about its provenance, but Lady Sophia did. Even Lady Jersey, who was perhaps the richest heiress in the kingdom, gushed about it.

She wondered if she should compliment them about their lovely dresses and the sparkling coronets they wore, but she was much too timid.

When the orchestra started, Adam claimed her for the first set. She was relieved that even if she made a misstep, he would understand. He never chided her because of her unsophisticated ways. Though she was nervous at first, she soon gained confidence. Not only that, she was extraordinarily proud to be standing up with the most handsome man present, extraordinarily proud to be his wife, and extraordinarily proud of her own appearance. It would have been impossible to have looked better than she did tonight. She had no illusions that she was a great beauty (as Maria most certainly was), but she was keenly aware of the role of a talented hairdresser, a skilled modiste, and nearly priceless jewels played in creating the illusion of beauty. She had Adam to thank for all of this.

And for so much more. As they danced, she reveled in her good fortune. If only there was some way she could repay his many kindnesses in some way. For now, all she could do was to make sure she did not embarrass him.

As they faced each other on the long way as another pair of dancers executed their steps between the two rows, the look her husband gave her was enough to melt her expanding heart. There was such tenderness in his warm gaze, she wanted to throw herself into his arms and kiss him.

After the first set was over, the three Birmingham brothers and their wives gathered for Almack's notoriously bland punch. Being with these new relations compensated for the trepidation of an unfamiliar situation. Not that her own nervousness in any way diminished her joy. She had never thought she, little Orphan Emma from Upper Barrington, would ever be standing in Almack's amongst so many aristocratic matrons whom she had read about for years. Never would she have thought to see so many stunning gowns or so many fabulous jewels.

"It's official," Lady Fiona said, gazing up adoringly at her husband, "Nick has filed his candidacy for Parliament."

"This is great news," William said.

Adam smiled at the brother who looked so much like him. "We'll do anything we can to help you."

"I'm gratified you said that." Nick's gaze circled the family gathering. "I need to do electioneering in Yorkshire later this week, and I can use some familial support."

"We'll come," Adam said.

Emma felt like whooping with joy. She would get to go to York! Even better—she was assured of many more days in his presence.

"I think all our lovely wives should come, too," William said. "Nick will be sure to win then."

Lady Sophia nodded vigorously. "My brother tells me that the voters do love to interact with candidates' pretty wives—not that I'm suggesting I'm pretty—but Lady Fiona and Emma most certainly are."

Will's gaze softened as he peered at his wife. "Any man with eyes in his head would know I have the good fortune to have wed the loveliest lady in the kingdom . . ." He paused and looked at Emma and Lady Fiona. "Meaning no offense to the other beautiful ladies present."

They all laughed.

"Since it's *your* electioneering," Adam said to

Nick, "I'll leave all the traveling arrangements to you. I will, of course bring my carriage."

Nick nodded. "Don't worry about servants. Mine can handle the six of us—your valet and your lady's maid excepted."

"There's no sense in coming in three carriages," William said. "Sophia and I can double up."

"Why don't you ride with Adam and Emma?" Lady Fiona suggested. "We'll be bringing Emmie—who's dying to see her Aunt Verity' babe. The dear child takes up a whole seat with all her dolls."

William shook his head. "No. Adam and Emma ride with me."

"I'd almost forgotten," Lady Fiona said with a little laugh, "how *well-suited* Will's carriage is for long-distance travel."

For her part, Emma could not believe William's carriage superior to Adam's. Nothing could be as comfortable as Adam's for a long ride.

Adam raised his brows and directed his remarks to his wife. "Because my youngest brother believes the Birminghams can be a target for robbers, he always travels with a veritable arsenal."

"And," Nick added, "he knows how to use the weapons."

Adam chuckled. "Mama always says the Lord makes the youngest son the toughest for a very good reason."

"How many days will the journey take?" Emma asked.

"If we leave very early," Nick said, "and if the roads are good, and if there's no rain, we should be able to make the trip in two very long days."

"Then we'd be one night at an inn on the

way?" Lady Sophia inquired.

Nick nodded.

It would be Emma's first time ever to stay at an inn. How exciting! Her face brightened as she looked up at her husband. "Then I shall get to meet Verity, too?"

Adam eyed her affectionately. "As well as our mother."

Would her adventures never cease? How thrilling that she would be seeing more of England that she had ever thought to see! How fun it would be to travel in William's fine coach, especially with her sweet sister-in-law, Lady Sophia. She also admired William vastly. How excited she was that she would meet Adam's sister and mother.

More excitement was to follow when the orchestra struck up the next set. Even though she thought she would rather be a spectator than a participant, alas, she discovered she was favored by a great many gentlemen here, judging by the rush of men begging her to stand up with them. She had no precedent for such an occurrence. Added to that quandary, she did not know one man from another.

Adam took the dilemma from her hands. "Lord Drummond," he said to the first man, "I should like to present my wife to you."

Lord Drummond, who was older even than Adam, eyed her. "I do pray, Mrs. Birmingham, you will do me the goodness of standing up with me."

* * *

Adam had no desire to dance with any woman other than his wife. In fact, he was compelled to stand at the wall and watch as she danced with Drummond. He had wanted to be proud of Emma.

He'd wanted her to look lovely in her new finery. But he had not been prepared for the way he felt when other men made cakes of themselves over *his* wife! Drummond was a notorious womanizer. Not at all the sort he wanted hanging about his sweet little wife. And Drummond wasn't the only one. Several noted rakes had been practically drooling over Emma as if she were fresh meat. He did not at all like the way the so-called cream of society conducted extramarital affairs.

Now there was still another reason he must look out for her welfare.

$\mathcal{C}$hapter 14

She was surprised the following morning when she entered the breakfast room to find Adam already there. "Sweet heavens, but you've actually arrived here first. How novel!"

He was seated at the table, a steaming cup of coffee in his hand, a plate piled with toast in front of him, and he was regarding her with a stern expression.

Her heart fell. After her success the previous night, she had hoped he would be proud of her.

"I have to go to the bank today."

Was that why he was so grave? Did he regret that they would not be able to spend the day together? She helped herself to coffee from the sideboard, slathered butter on a slice of toast, and came to sit across from him. "I shall miss you."

"I expect you'll be besieged with morning callers today," he said gruffly.

"But I talked with no woman, other than Lady Fiona and Lady Sophia. I did greet Lady Jersey and Lady Cowper, but I hardly think women of their stature will be calling on me."

His eyes narrowed. "I'm not talking about women. Men will come calling today. Expect to receive nosegays."

Her eyes widened. "You can't be serious! They all know I'm a married woman."

"That has never stood in the way of the *flirtations* carried on by men in the *ton*."

"What can I do to discourage flirtations?"

"Nothing. But I must warn you. Many of those men who clamored to dance with you last night are not honorable men. If they call on you, you must be civil to them. But never, ever allow yourself to be alone with any of them. Ever."

She was stunned. "I'm not quite certain I understand what you're saying, understand your warning. Are you saying that peers of the realm with lovely wives and families would try to steal another man's wife?"

"Not steal."

Her brows lowered. "Do you mean they would find it acceptable to, say, drive around Hyde Park with a woman other than their own wife?"

He cleared his throat. "Nothing so public. In fact, some of these men boast about . . . bedding married women."

She could feel the heat climbing into her cheeks. Her mouth went dry. Her eyes locked with his. Even though he was her husband, she was embarrassed to speak on such a personal topic in front of him. She wanted to say, "There's only one man I would ever bed, and that is my husband." But, she was too shy. Finally she said, "Surely you know I am not that kind of woman."

He nodded solemnly. "It's just that many people, especially ones who have never lived in glittering Society, are often so humbled in the presence of nobility they consent to things they never would have done with a mere mister."

Her embarrassment turned to anger. She put hands to hips and glared at him. "I may be unsophisticated, sir, but I am neither stupid nor immoral." She leapt from her chair and stormed from the chamber.

Cursing under his breath, he rushed after her, kicking his chair to the floor as he did so. He was faster than she. When she was half way up the stairs he came abreast of her and gripped her arm. "Forgive me."

She spun around to face him, her eyes still flashing with fury.

He let go of her arm. "I never thought you were anything but principled. You've done nothing wrong. It is my mind which has latched onto this vile subject." He drew a deep breath. "I . . . I was angered by Drummond's attentions to you. I was so proud of your beauty . . . until I realized other men would wish to claim you." He shrugged and offered a wan smile. "I have found that I don't fancy sharing you."

If she weren't certain he was in love with Maria, she would have thought Adam was jealous. At the notion, her anger vanished. She touched his arm. "I pledged myself to but one man before God, the priest, and your family. One man only. Always and forever."

His black eyes were inscrutable as he peered down at her. A muscle in his angular face twitched. He swallowed. Then he did something curious. He lifted her hand and placed a kiss upon it.

Her heart exploded. It wasn't the kiss on her lips that she had prayed for, but it was wonderful nevertheless.

"I wish I didn't have to go to the bank today, but since we'll be traveling to Yorkshire tomorrow I have to dispatch some duties before we leave."

A soft smile on her face, she nodded. "If any of

those dreadful peers should call upon me, I shall regale them with praises of my husband."

He smiled and offered his arm. "Please join me for breakfast."

* * *

To her astonishment, Lord Drummond did call on her not long after Adam departed for The City. And her husband had been right. Lord Drummond presented her with a nosegay of violets encased in lovely white lace.

Entertaining morning callers was another new experience for which she was ill prepared. What did one do? "Please sit down, my lord." She waved toward a slender-legged French chair near the silken sofa where she sat. She had no notion of how to begin a conversation with this man. She did not admire him in the least since she had learned he was blatantly unfaithful to his wife. She held the bouquet in her hand. When Studewood entered the chamber she would ask him to see that it was placed in water. "The flowers are lovely. How thoughtful of you." Her voice lacked sincerity. All she could think of was Adam's warning not to allow herself to be alone with this man. Would this be considered being *alone*? The house was, after all, filled with servants.

She felt tainted just by sitting in the same chamber as him. What a pity that Therese had been dispatched on an errand for her. Otherwise, Therese could have sat in this chamber to lend propriety.

"Lovely flowers for a lovely lady. Tell me, Mrs. Birmingham, how is it that I have never before seen you?"

"I have spent my entire life in a small village,

my lord."

His sultry gaze lazily trailed over her, pausing discernibly on her breasts. "Birmingham is most fortunate to have captured you *before* you came upon the *ton.*"

This line of conversation must stop. "It is I who am the fortunate one. Every minute of the day I count my blessings that my dear husband chose me for his wife."

Lord Drummond's eyes narrowed. "Spoken like a bride."

She was thankful Studewood had kept the room's door open. She kept eyeing it, hopeful that Studewood would return. She would be mortified if Adam learned she was alone with this noted scoundrel. Finally she strode to the bell pull and yanked it. "I fear my beautiful flowers will wilt if we don't put them in water."

Studewood came promptly and she asked him to see to her flowers. "Then please bring them back. I do so love violets." In reality, she didn't prefer violets over other flowers, but the more often she was not alone with Lord Drummond, the less agitated she would be. And, hopefully, the presence of others would prevent his unwelcome overtures.

"Since you are new to London, Mrs. Birmingham, it would give me great pleasure to show you about my city."

"How very kind of you," she said without enthusiasm, "but we are now preparing for a trip to Yorkshire for my brother Nicholas's electioneering."

"Oh, yes, I heard where he was standing for Parliament. A pity he's pledged himself to the Whigs."

She was grasping for any topic that would get his mind off wanting to be alone with her. "Then I take it you're a Tory, my lord?"

"Indeed I am. My family has always aligned ourselves with Tories. Those of us who support our Crown are Tories."

"The aunt who raised me greatly admired the Tories."

"An intelligent woman, to be sure."

Having apparently exhausted the Parliamentary topic, they sat silent for a moment. Her ears strained when she thought she heard a door closing , followed by voices downstairs in the entry hall.

"I daresay the loveliest woman at Almack's last night will be holding court today," he said.

She gave him a quizzing look. "To whom can you be referring, my lord?"

He laughed. "You, my dear lady, were the loveliest woman at the assembly."

"It's very kind of you to say that, my lord, but I strenuously disagree. Your opinion is influenced by my novelty—and the lovely dresses and jewels my husband's fortune has procured."

"Not true."

Footsteps sounded on the stairs, and seconds later Lady Sophia, swathed in soft rose, swept into the room. Her gaze riveted to Emma's visitor. "Lord Drummond, I see your reputation is intact for ingratiating yourself with . . . fresh beauty."

Before he could respond, she moved to Emma and kissed her cheek. "How lovely you look today, my dear sister."

When she sat next to Emma, Emma could have curtseyed before her in gratitude.

"I was pleasantly surprised to find you home

today. Adam's been devoting every moment since you married to showing you London." Lady Sophia eyed the earl. "Her husband is besotted."

Lord Drummond met Lady Sophia's gaze with amusement. "What's not to besot?"

Lady Sophia turned to Emma. "It forcefully struck me this morning that you must be presented to the queen."

Emma could have swooned. Was meeting the queen an honor accorded to a non-aristocrat? "Are you sure that is something I could be permitted to do?"

"I would be happy to sponsor you," Lord Drummond said.

Lady Sophia glared at him. "No need, my lord. My brother has already done so. I just left him."

The very idea of getting to meet the queen lifted Emma's gloom. "I could wear the lavender dress I wore last night!"

"No." Lady Sophia shook her head. "As beautiful as that dress is, it will not do for court. Court dresses are . . . well, more old fashioned. The skirts are quite full. You should see mine. There's enough fabric in it to drape every window in our house."

"Surely you exaggerate."

Lady Sophia laughed. "A little, but I believe I made my point."

Lord Drummond rose. "I must take my leave, ladies. It's been a pleasure." He bowed over their gloved hands for a mock kiss then left.

Once he was gone, Emma whispered her thanks to her sister. "I cannot tell you how much I prayed that someone else would call on me. Adam did not want me to be alone with that horrid man, but I didn't know what to do."

"Adam has every right to be angered at him. Drummond is probably the most dishonorable man in all of London. But you did nothing wrong. Was he trying to get you away from here?"

"He told me he wanted to show me *his* city, but I told him we were preparing for our journey to Yorkshire."

"You did well. Were you able to think of a way to discourage him?"

Emma shrugged. "I thickly laid on the praise of my husband."

"Good girl." Lady Sophia sighed. "Those other men from Almack's last night will be sure to call on you today, too. Will that bother you?"

"It will. There's only one man I want to be with."

"It's the same with me and William," Lady Sophia said in a soft voice. "Why don't you and I go see about getting your court dress made? You use Madame De Guerney, do you not?"

"Yes. Do you?"

"No."

An awkward silence followed. Of course Lady Sophia would know Adam had taken her to Madame De Guerney because that's who Maria had used.

For the first time in her life, Emma was consumed with jealousy—toward a woman she had never met.

She ought to be grateful to the Italian opera singer. Her rejection brought about Emma's happiness.

* * *

Lady Sophia's sage counsel at Madame De Guerney's was greatly appreciated. They spent an hour there selecting the silk and all the adornments for the presentation dress. "I never

would have known what to do without you,"
Emma told her as they returned to Sophia's
carriage.

"It was my pleasure. I love anything to do with
fashion."

The coachman cleared his throat. "I thought,
my lady, you might want know that ever since we
left Mr. Adam's house, we've been followed by a
man on a horse."

"How singular," Lady Sophia said. "Watch
carefully as we return and let us know if you see
him again."

"Do you have any reason to believe anyone
would be following you?" Lady Sophia asked
Emma once they were facing each other in the
coach.

Emma shrugged. "I don't, but I should probably
tell you—in the strictest confidence—that we
believe my uncle was murdered."

"Dear Lord, that's terrible! Do you know who
the murderer is?"

"We think it's the man named heir in my
uncle's last will—which we believe was forged."

"How frightening, yet fascinating! Does he know
you suspect him?"

"I'm not sure. He does know I have challenged
the will, so he probably knows I suspect the will
was forged. Since he's not possessed of a high
degree of intelligence, it's unlikely he realizes that
I have strong suspicions my uncle was murdered."

"What a vile man. Will you permit me to share
this intelligence with William?"

"Of course. It's just not something we want
widely known at this time."

"It's the sort of thing that excites William
frightfully. He adores living dangerously."

"Which must terrify you."

"Indeed it does, but since we want to have children, he knows he had to stop risking his neck."

"How long have you been married?"

"Six months. I have hopes you and I will be breeding at the same time. How much fun it will be for the cousins!"

Nothing would make Emma happier, but the very mention of it plunged her into gloom. If only she and Adam had a *normal* marriage. "It would be lovely."

"Has Adam bought you your own carriage yet?"

"No. There's been no need. I've been blessed to spend every day with him since we've married."

Lady Sophia sighed. "Adam must be deeply in love."

"I wish I could say it was my presence that's kept us together so much, but to be honest he's obsessed over bringing my uncle's murderer to justice."

"It's a wonder Adam went to the bank today."

"Since we'll leave for Yorkshire tomorrow, he had many duties that couldn't be put off ."

"Still, you have been blessed to have him with you so much. I would rather spend my days with William than buy jewels at Rundell and Bridge."

"I feel the same about Adam," Emma said, her voice barely above a whisper.

When they arrived at Curzon Street, she stopped and spoke to Lady Sophia's coachman. "Did you see that man on the horse again?"

"No, madam."

How curious. She wondered if she should tell Adam about it, but decided against it. He might think she was being stalked by Lord Drummond.

The less said on such a topic, the better. She was flattered that Adam seemed jealous, but she did not want to do anything that would arouse his anger.

$\mathcal{C}$hapter 15

It was impossible to suppress the smile on her face. Emma's journey up north was a thousand times more joyful than her recent journey *from* the north—and that one had heretofore been the most exciting thing she had ever done. Not that her first journey had actually been exciting, given that the post chaise was uncomfortably crowded. She was forced to share her seat with a very large man who obviously shunned bathing and whose gargantuan belly rested upon his thighs. Her eager anticipation of London and all its attractions, though, easily compensated for any of the trip's discomforts.

But today's journey in William's luxurious coach was so pleasurable she not only was oblivious to the cold, she also found herself wishing they would never reach Yorkshire. Riding in a carriage with Adam always pleased her. She thought perhaps her deep satisfaction had more to do with her husband's close proximity than with the comfort of the conveyance, though she must own she had never ridden upon seats as comfortable as the plush velvet ones in the Birmingham carriages. As had become his custom, Adam sat next to her, just as William sat next to Lady Sophia across from them.

It was comforting, too, that she and Adam

would be together every minute for the next several days. She fleetingly wondered if there was anything she could do to make him forget Maria, if there was anything she could do to capture his heart. Inexperienced in the ways of courtship, she came to the conclusion she was incapable of manipulating his heart. The only things she could control were her own actions. She could be agreeable, act intelligently, and try not to be an embarrassment to him.

It was also exciting to share their ride with Will and the lovely Lady Sophia. As an only child, Emma had always longed for siblings. And now she had them. She treasured having sisters-in-law and brothers-in-law and rejoiced in how openly they had welcomed her into their family.

She was especially grateful to Lady Sophia for the many ways she had helped her. How honored she was to have one of Lady's Sophia's social stature, unerring taste, and extraordinary beauty as her . . . friend. Adam had told her that before she wed Will, half the peers in the kingdom had begged for her hand in marriage.

Whenever Emma was with her, she studied every accessory, every cut of every dress, every nuance of the lady's silky voice. Emma could barely remove her gaze from William's beautiful wife. Today Lady Sophia wore a red velvet cloak over an ivory traveling dress. With her dark tresses, she stunned in red.

"Do you know what William saw in the *Morning Chronicle* today?" Lady Sophia asked.

Adam met her amused gaze. "Are you referring to the announcement of Nick's candidacy?"

Lady Sophia stomped her well-shod foot. "You, dear Adam, are stealing my thunder!"

"Sorry. Allow me to start over. Do, Lady Sophia, tell us what William found in the *Chronicle* this morning."

William chuckled.

Lady Sophia directed her attention at Emma. "Not only did the article announce that Nick is standing for Parliament, but it enumerated all the Whig leaders who have endorsed him. All of London will be talking about our Nicholas Birmingham."

"I think it's lovely that all the prominent Whigs have so enthusiastically praised him," Emma said.

Adam nodded. "Yes, Mr. Lamb and Lord John Russell have both championed him."

"They're not only powerful Whigs," William said, "they're smart. They are well aware of Nick's strengths—as they should be. He will be a huge asset to them."

"Having very deep pockets is also very useful," Adam added.

"It is a pity women are not allowed to vote," Lady Sophia said.

Emma nodded, smiling. "Yes, a man that handsome would handily win." She

then lifted the curtain to peer from her window. "How fortunate we are that the roads are good. No rain. No menacing clouds in the sky."

Lady Sophia grimaced and scooted closer to her husband. "Just blustery winds and bitter cold."

"We'll probably only have to spend one night at an inn," Adam said.

Her heartbeat accelerated. Adam had told her that, like Nick and William with their wives, he and Emma would share a bedchamber. "I give you my word I will behave as a gentleman," he had vowed.

She didn't want him to be a gentleman; she wanted him to be a lover. But she was far too shy to give voice to her deepest longings. Not only that, she feared that after lying with the no-doubt voluptuous Maria, he would never be attracted to a woman like her. Emma's new finery was all that kept her from looking like a girl barely old enough to leave the schoolroom. Nevertheless, the very idea of sleeping upon the same bed as him filled her with a sense of bliss.

Several times that day William had addressed his wife as Isadore. After the fourth time, Emma summoned the courage to ask, "Pray, William, why do you refer to Lady Sophia as Isadore?"

Lady Sophia's dark eyes met her husband's, and both laughed. "It is because when I met this vixen she did nothing but lie to me—particularly about her name."

Emma's eyes rounded. "She told you her name was Isadore?"

"I did," Lady Sophia said.

"I had been told a beautiful woman named Isadore would be contacting me, and when this . . . " William's simmering gaze locked with his wife's, "this beautiful pseudo trollop strode up to me and said she'd been waiting for me, I quite naturally thought she had to be Isadore."

"My husband was meeting this woman to conduct illegal business, so you can only guess what sort of woman the real Isadore was."

Adam turned to Emma to explain further. "Before Lady Sophia tamed our brother, he was never happy unless he was breaking the law or endangering himself."

"My greatest offense was smuggling gold bullion illegally into the country—a practice I have since abandoned."

Emma didn't know what to say. She directed her attention to Lady Sophia. "How long did you pretend to be Isadore?"

"A few weeks."

"And," William added, "she instructed her maid to pretend to be her mute sister."

Lady Sophia shrugged. "If she had spoken, he would have known she couldn't be my sister. That's why I forced her to portray a mute. It was really clever of me to keep my elder sister with me at all times to protect me from this unscrupulous man."

William took his wife's hand. "Even believing she was my Shady Lady, I still fell in love with Isadore."

"I think that's very romantic," Emma said. She recalled Adam telling her that two of his siblings had fallen in love with members of the aristocracy without knowing their true identities. "Adam told me that Verity, too, fell in love with Lord Agar without knowing his identity."

Lady Sophia sighed. "And they are so much in love still. You will get the opportunity to see them for yourself."

"I greatly look forward to it."

"Have you told Adam about your presentation?" Lady Sophia asked.

Emma turned to her husband. "Did you know Lord Devere has sponsored my presentation?"

"That's wonderful."

"And Lady Sophia was kind enough to take me to Madame De Guerney's for her to create my gown. I hope that's all right with you."

He chuckled as he placed his arm around her, drawing her even closer to him. "You know I will refuse you nothing, dear one."

Lady Sophia rolled her eyes. "I declare, Adam, you're every bit as besotted as Lord Agar is over Verity."

"He and I are most fortunate," Adam said.

If only he meant it.

"Selecting Emma's dress rescued your dear wife from having to entertain those odious callers like Lord Drummond."

Adam stiffened. His brows lowered. "Did Drummond call?" he asked Emma, his voice icy.

She solemnly nodded.

"You have no fears," Lady Sophia said, "that just because Emma's inexperienced in ways of the *ton* that she would preen under Drummond's attentions. She could barely tolerate the horrid man and was only barely civil to him. We couldn't get out of there too soon. The last thing your wife wanted was to sit there with lecherous men of that sort."

"Then you were there?" he asked Lady Sophia.

"Yes. And I stressed how much you two love each other."

Emma could feel her cheeks burning.

He took Emma's hand and spoke softly. "I'm happy you and Lady Sophia found a way to extricate you from having to be with that man."

She smiled. "I get very vexed with that bank of yours. I would rather have *you* with me day and night."

"You shall learn—as Lady Fiona has—that you must share your husband with a mistress. A mistress that's a brick building," Will said.

"I cannot wait to commiserate with Lady Fiona." Emma wondered if Adam would know she spoke the truth, or would he think she was playacting to convince others theirs was a normal marriage.

"As grateful as I am to Lady Sophia for taking you to Madame De Guerney's, I can see that it's time you got your own carriage, my dear one."

She pouted. "I much prefer having you take me everywhere I need to go." She was almost certain her husband would think she was portraying a devoted wife. Little did he know she really was a devoted wife.

He squeezed her hand, and she thought her heart would explode. "As much as I wish it, you know that our daytime contact will soon be coming to an end." Adam must be mimicking her supposed playacting.

As soon as the situation with her uncle's death was resolved, Adam would never again spend his days with her. Was the most exciting part of her life to be over when she reached one-and-twenty? It was a bitter thought.

* * *

As much as he enjoyed sharing the coach with Lady Sophia and William, he was happy when they ran out of topics to discuss, and a peaceful lull settled over them. Lady Sophia finally succumbed to the involuntary closing of her lids, put her head on William's shoulder, and went to sleep with her husband's arm around her.

Adam felt strangely compelled to place his arm around Emma again. How could such a small female overpower a big fellow like him with such a surge of emotions? Since the moment of their meeting, he'd felt the need to take care of her. But now those feelings of serving as her protector dominated him like he'd once been dominated by Maria's sensuousness.

Yet when he held Emma's slim body close, he

had come to desire her in the same way he'd desired Maria—yet it was entirely different.

Whatever he'd felt for Maria had been purely physical. What he felt for Emma was pure. One's wife was a completely different creature than one's mistress.

But, of course, he would love Maria for as long as he drew breath. These feelings Emma elicited were merely a response to his craving for Maria.

He tenderly watched as Emma's lids grew heavy. That was all it took. He drew her close and found himself placing soft kisses on top of her head. Soon she was asleep.

Holding her felt so good.

He was the only one in the coach still awake. Afternoon darkened to night, and the wheels of the carriage kept rattling over the North Road, chilled air filling the carriage. He wondered how much longer they would ride. They'd been in the carriage for fourteen hours with only short breaks.

His question was soon answered when their coach pulled alongside of Nick's, and the coachmen exchanged the information that they would stop for the night in the next village which had a suitable inn.

Everyone came awake and sat up straight. He was disappointed to forfeit the feel of his youthful wife in his arms.

In less than ten minutes, their carriage pulled into the innyard. The winds battered the swinging sign for the Golden Fleece. He'd worried that because it was so late, there would be no rooms available but was pleasantly surprised that only two other coaches had arrived before them.

* * *

In her entire twenty years Emma had never

before been inside of a coaching inn, but she hardly wanted her companions to know the extent of her inexperience. As it was, she had little opportunity to observe the establishment's public areas. Once Nick's man procured three chambers for "members of the Quality," all them were whisked upstairs to a generous parlor attached to a large corner bedchamber. She quickly saw that they would eat at a table in this room—far away from those of the lower classes who ate and drank in the tavern below.

Because a thatched roof crowned the whitewashed inn, Emma had pictured its rooms as a low-ceilinged rabbit warren, but that was not the case. Though the ceilings were lower than what she was accustomed to, these two rooms were exceptionally large. Sputtering fires in the hearths were already warming the chambers.

Before they could divest themselves of cloaks and hats, two young serving maids brought them ale and a pot of hot tea. The same girls returned with plates, utensils, and hot food before the six of them had taken their seats around the table.

Emma watched as the famished Birmingham brothers attacked their mutton. Everyone was so busy easting, no one spoke the first five minutes of dinner. It had been nearly eight hours since they had last eaten.

Emma gazed into the adjoining bedchamber and froze. Lady Fiona's maid was securing her mistress's fine linens upon the room's big tester bed.

Was it a huge *faux pas* if a member of the Quality forgot to bring one's own linens? Her stomach sank. She completely lost her appetite. How humiliated she would be in front of her husband when he learned that her incompetence would force them to sleep on inferior bedding. Dear God, what if it wasn't clean? She was mortified.

She fleetingly hoped that her own maid would be seeing to the placement of fresh Birmingham linens upon the bed she and Adam (this thought accompanied by a frenzied fluttering of her heart) would sleep upon. But dear Therese was as much of a novice in the homes of the wealthy as Emma was.

Only when Adam finished his plate did he notice she wasn't touching her food. "Do you not like the food, dear one?"

She shrugged. "It gives no offense. It's just that I seem to have lost my appetite."

"I daresay one as small as our Emma doesn't require great amounts of food," Lady Fiona said.

"She usually eats more than this," Adam snapped. "Are you unwell, my dearest?"

She was touched over his concern. *It will probably be the last time*—once her shortcomings began to amass like timber on a bonfire. It was only a matter of time before he would loathe her and repent this marriage with every breath he drew.

"Perhaps she has a touch of carriage sickness," Nick offered.

William shook his head. "She was quite well throughout our journey."

"Yes," Lady Sophia agreed. "Her colour was good."

Why was everyone talking about her as if she weren't there?

Adam kept looking at her, concern etched on his handsome face.

She could hardly explain the source of her moroseness. Her own ignorance was ruining everything. The family gathering she had so greatly looked forward to in the inn's intimate setting had suddenly turned into a nightmare. Now all she wanted to do was isolate herself from what was sure to be disapproving glances.

I don't belong. The words ran through her mind like the fragment of a favorite song. As kind as these people were, they must find her an embarrassment.

Her gaze lifted to Adam's. "I think I need to go to . . . our chamber."

He leapt to his feet. "I'll accompany you."

She shook her head. "I am capable of finding it."

"Whether you're capable or not, I'm coming." He snatched her arm.

As he guided her along the narrow, wood-floored corridor, she trembled, and tears gathered in her eyes. She had best confess before he discovered her unforgivable omission. She stopped beneath the wall sconce but did not look up at him. She did not want him to see how moist her eyes were. "I must warn you that I have failed most miserably."

"How, my dear wife, have you failed?"

"I did not know about bringing the linens. I've never stayed at an inn. Until this month, I had never traveled anywhere. I'm am sadly incompetent to be your wife, and I understand if you wish to . . . "

He started laughing.

"Pray, sir, what amuses you so?"

"My very own dear one, you will find our bed dressed in the finest linens that can be procured."

"But . . . "

"Traveling accommodations are not the concern of the mistress of the house. That is why we engage competent servants. My man saw to everything. He's taken your young maid under his wing, too, to explain the ways of a household such as ours."

All the tension in her body uncoiled. She giggled. "You cannot imagine how upset I was when I saw Lady Fiona's maid dressing their bed. I was quite certain my ignorance was a mortifying embarrassment to you."

He lifted her chin and smiled. "Never that."

They continued on to their chamber. It was actually two small, connected chambers like Nick's and Lady Fiona's but smaller. A blazing wood fire was lighted in the hearth, and Therese was placing a candle at the bedside table in the adjoining room. A quick glance there confirmed that fresh linens of high quality had been placed on the canopied bed.

"It's so refreshing to smell wood burning after the nasty coals of London," he said.

"Wood fires are likely the only thing I miss from Upper Barrington."

He yawned. "I'm actually happy you wanted to come to bed before the others. I feel as exhausted as one who's been chopping wood all day."

She started to giggle again. "When, my dear husband, have you ever chopped wood?"

A crooked grin lopped across his face. "I don't suppose I ever have."

"I do understand your meaning. Sitting in a coach all day is very wearying."

"I'll leave to allow your maid to get you ready for bed. Expect me back in ten minutes. Ready for sleep."

Her pulse thundered as she watched him walk away.

Chapter 16

"Which would you wear if you wanted to look ravishing to your husband—if you had a husband?" Emma asked Therese.

Her maid flung aside a soft woolen night shift, walked straight to Emma's smart new valise, and plucked out a night shift of snowy white linen nearly as thin and soft as gossamer. "You will be most beautiful in this, madame, and Mr. Birmingham, he will be captivated by your beauty."

She obviously embellished to please her mistress. Emma drew a deep breath. She was still trembling in anticipation of sharing this chamber with Adam. "Then please help me to dazzle." *A pity I will never be as desirable as Maria.*

After she was dressed for sleeping and Therese had departed, Emma climbed onto the bed and buried herself beneath the blankets. In spite of the fire that warmed the chamber, her thin linen shift offered little protection against the chills seeping into the room from the multi-paned window.

She would not blow out the candle. Once he made his way to their bed, he could do so. *Their bed.* The very thought of it was more intoxicating than bubbling French champagne. Her breasts felt heavy, and there was a tingling low in her torso—

alien yet surprisingly pleasing feelings.

Should she happily greet him when entered the chamber? Or should she pretend to be sleepy? Because he had given her his word, she knew he would not initiate any intimacies this night.

Would it be possible for her to ignite feelings of passion in him? She gave a bitter laugh. One who looked as youthful as she was hardly likely to induce passionate feelings in any man who was accustomed to lying with a . . . practiced mistress.

Adam was certain to say good-night, roll over, and go to sleep. She smiled when she recalled that first night when he'd dropped to her chaise and promptly fallen into a brandy-aided slumber. She could still hear his snores.

A man's snoring had shocked her that first night. Now she craved to be able to hear Adam's.

Her heart hammered when she heard a man's footsteps coming along the corridor. They stopped at their door. He entered the parlor, then lightening his footfall, came into the bedchamber.

She sat up.

"Oh, you're still awake."

She giggled. "It's only been ten minutes! I'm incapable of falling into an instant sleep—like someone I happen to know."

He came to the other side of the bed, sat on it with his back to her, and began to remove his boots. "Will you always remember me as that debilitatingly stupid drunk?"

"Of course. He was very nice to me."

"I could have badly tarnished your good reputation."

"One only has a reputation when one knows people. I didn't know a single soul in London."

"You would never have allowed your anonymity

to relax your morals, nor would I have allowed it." He came to his feet. "I'm going to blow out the candle, remove my breeches, and climb into the bed."

* * *

She'd been partially right about his ability to fall asleep instantly. Normally—even without brandy—he fell asleep within seconds of lying down. But not tonight. He'd turned his back to her in an attempt to diminish her effect upon him. For in spite of his vow, he kept thinking about her in the most provocative way.

A full fifteen minutes after he had lain down, she whispered, "You're not asleep yet?"

"Nor are you." He kept picturing her ivory shoulders and the trace of her nipples beneath the soft linen of her night shift. How lovely she had looked in the dim glow of their room's only candle. He wanted to kiss her. He wanted to weigh her breasts within his hands. He wanted to feel himself within her.

" I know it's not exciting for an experienced man like you, but I'm so excited to be sharing a bed with my husband that I cannot go to sleep."

"Pray, what's so exciting?"

She sighed. "The intimacy, I suppose. I've never before been close to another as I am with you. Would you mind terribly if I said you're my best friend?"

The notion warmed him in the same way his mother's caress did when he was a feverish lad. He could not help but to recall Nick telling him that Lady Fiona was his best friend as well as his lover, then William telling him the same thing about Lady Sophia after they had wed.

"Of course I wouldn't mind. I'm flattered." A pity

he couldn't tell her he felt the same. The fact was he had only thought of her in a rather paternal sense. But these past two days she had become much less of a child and much more of a woman to him.

And she had become the object of his desire.

His present arousal was evidence of that. He throbbed with his need for her. But it was a need he would not act upon. He feigned a yawn.

"Good-night, my dearest," she said.

God, but he wanted to draw her into his arms. "Good-night, dear one."

It was many hours before he fell asleep. Because her breathing never changed, he knew she, too, was unable to sleep.

They would feel as if they were at death's door tomorrow.

* * *

Nick had informed them the previous night that they would leave the inn just as the sun was rising. Emma wasn't alone in stifling her yawns as the carriage sped through the murky dawn. She was well aware that Adam also had difficulty falling asleep. Unlike her, whose every thought had been about him, he was probably worrying about how his bank was managing without him.

Though she'd been exhausted and had craved sleep all through the night, she would gladly repeat the night to once more share the cozy bedchamber with Adam. How fortunate were married couples who could sleep each night with their loved one.

It did not escape her notice that Lady Sophia's hand, swathed in red gloves today, rested in William's. Both of them looked so utterly content.

"How many nights will we be at Lord and Lady

Agar's?" Emma asked.

William's brows lowered. "You didn't know?"

"Know what?"

"Nick's decided he can't be away from the Exchange for that long," William said.

She wondered how he would manage attending Parliamentary sessions, but Adam had said those typically did not start before four in the afternoon. "The aristocrats, I am told, seldom rise before noon," he told her. She thought sleeping a terrible waste of daylight.

Adam touched her forearm. "I hope you're not too disappointed."

"While I *am* disappointed, I'm grateful that I'll be able to meet your mother and Verity." Emma's eyes narrowed. She faced her husband. "I shall be obliged to address her as Lady Agar instead of Verity, will I not? What do you fellows call your sister?"

"Verity," they both said at once.

"Do you never say to other people *my sister, Lady Agar*?" Emma asked.

Both brothers laughed. "It sounds . . . pompous, I suppose," Adam said. "I've never been one to crave connections with the aristocracy." He turned to Lady Sophia. "Not to disparage your class, my dear lady. I am very happy to be connected to you."

Lady Sophia started to giggle.

"I picture Verity in much the same way I picture Ladies Fiona and Sophia," Emma said. "Impeccable taste and manners with a confident and gracious air about her."

The brothers locked gazes. William's brow rose. "Do you think your wife's off the mark?" he asked Adam.

Adam nodded. "Most certainly. Verity is . . . Verity. She's not at all like her brothers."

Lady Sophia raised a hand. "Except she is possessed of an unerring eye—as are all the Birmingham brothers."

"True," William agreed. "But our sister is shy. She is the anomaly of a woman of very few words."

Lady Sophia poked her husband in the ribs.

"And despite that she's pretty, always beautifully dressed, and highly intelligent, she gives the impression that she lacks confidence," Adam said.

William nodded at each word Adam had said. "You have perfectly described our sister."

Emma understood. Despite all the advantages of the wealth she was born into, Verity would naturally have felt self-conscious among the nobility. Even if she had joined their ranks.

"The Agars and your mother will join us at the electioneering assembly?" Emma asked.

"Yes. Verity's keen for us to see her baby," William said.

"And our mother, who neither expresses herself nor shows emotion, wouldn't miss the opportunity to see Nick standing upon the stage."

William agreed with Adam. "She would never speak of how proud she is of Nick, but don't think that she's not! I've always thought she had a soft spot for her firstborn."

"I have, too," Adam said, "but she'll never admit it."

Lady Sophia directed her attention to Emma. "Don't be put off by the woman's chilliness. That's just her way."

That comment was met with more nods.

"Actually we're to assemble in Stenson Keyes,

at the assembly rooms there tomorrow morning," Will said. "That's where Mama and the Agars will come. For them, it is only a two-hour ride."

"Nicks says we should make the town's inn around nine tonight—if the roads stay good," Lady Sophia added.

Another night at an inn! Emma would love it.

* * *

The inn in Stenson Keyes was vastly different than the Golden Fleece. It was much larger and much newer. No half-timbered walls or thatched roof here. The u-shaped building of gray stone offered a huge livery stable, and the tavern area of the Blue Roost comprised several chambers, each with a blazing wood fire.

They ate good and plentiful food in their own private chamber on the ground floor before the exhausted travelers walked up the wooden staircase to their rooms. First was Nick's and Lady Fiona's, then Adam's and Emma's, then William's and Lady Sophia's.

Because they had all come up at the same time, it would have been awkward for Adam to hold back until his wife got dressed for bed. When they entered the chamber, he dismissed Therese.

When she was gone, he said, "I will turn my back while you prepare for bed." He then turned around and faced the door they had just entered.

As Emma removed her stockings, she kept telling herself he wasn't going to see her bare legs or her bare anything, but she was still embarrassed to be disrobing just feet away from a man. Even if that man was her husband.

It was also beastly cold.

Her heart thumped erratically and a chill surged through her like icy water when her dress and shift sifted to the floor and she stood there in only her stays and drawers. She attempted to unlace the stays in the back, but it was impossible. What was she to do?

She *could* ask Adam to help. It wasn't as if he had never done such a thing before. She would wager that her husband had frequently taken off Maria's garments. The thought of Adam removing her own clothing made Emma's breath ragged.

Until Maria intruded on her thoughts. How she detested the woman!

She fiddled with the same night shift she'd worn the previous night. She was trying to summon the courage to ask for Adam's help.

"What the devil is taking you so long?"

She cleared her throat. "I have a problem."

"Oh, God. It's your stays."

"Yes."

Now he cleared his throat. "I can help. You mustn't be embarrassed. I'll stay behind you. I won't look at your . . ." He stopped himself. "I'll just stay behind and unlace you."

"I trust you."

He turned.

Their gazes met. His gaze dropped to skim over her.

She coloured. In a good way. As embarrassed as she was, she felt womanly, and that was most certainly to be desired.

He jerked his gaze away. "Well, if you'll just turn around, I shall get about my business."

She presented her back to him, and he moved to her. As the laces began to loosen, it suddenly occurred to her that when it released her breasts, they would be completely exposed.

If he were in front of her.

She began to tremble.

The stays lowered. Her breasts sprung free. She swallowed.

"There now." He spoke as if he'd just fed his dog.

How could he be so casual when she felt as if she would explode with all these strange-but-wonderful feelings that threatened to overpower her?

Her hands trembling, face flaming, she quickly disrobed, snatched her night rail and shimmied into it. "You can turn around now."

He slowly turned. His gaze flicked to her, then he diverted his attentions to the other side of the bed from her. He sat on the bed, his back to her as he began to remove his boots.

"Do men not wear night shirts?" she asked.

One boot thumped to the wooden floor. He turned to face her. "Some do. My mother made all of us when we were lads, but as we grew older . . . well, I suppose men tend to get hot when they're beneath blankets. We don't wear . . . much."

"Like last night? I noticed you only slept in your breeches. No shirt. I would have been cold."

"The breeches were for your benefit."

"I don't un-," she stopped, her eyes widening. "Do you mean . . . ?"

"This subject is not fit for a maiden's ears."

She wanted to cry out that she was a wife, a married woman, but she was too timid. She slipped beneath the covers.

Moments later, he did the same, dousing the candle as he did so. "I shall sleep like the dead tonight."

"It was very difficult to keep one's eyes open throughout the coach ride today," she said. "It seemed that every churn of the wheel was contriving to make me sleepy."

"I felt the same. I will have no problem sleeping tonight."

"I believe I should like to have a good-night kiss from you."

He groaned. "Absolutely not."

His words could have shattered her, but there was a lightness in his tone that surprised her. "Then you don't wish to be my best friend."

"Best friends don't kiss."

"Then what about wives?"

"It's not as if you're actually . . ."

"Your wife." She pouted. "I promise I will endeavor to learn to be a good kisser. I know I was mammothly disappointing that first time."

"I don't wish to discuss kissing. I want to sleep."

His words wounded. She wouldn't even say good-night to him if he was going to be such an ogre.

* * *

She was in a deep sleep when a pounding sound awakened her. Her brain was too foggy to determine what the noise was or where it came from. Cursing, Adam left their bed, stumbled to the door, and cracked it open.

Who would be disturbing them at this hour? She bolted up in her bed, gathering the blankets to cover her shoulders.

"So sorry to be disturbing you, sir," a woman said, "but a gent in the tavern says it's prodigiously important that he speak to you at once."

"You must have the wrong room."

"Yer Mr. Birming'am? Mr. Adam Birming'am?"

"That's right."

"'E said 'e's come from Lunnon. Something important about yer bank."

Adam cursed again. "I'll be right down."

Judging by how much the logs in their hearth had burned, she would estimate it must be around midnight. The candlelight flickered on Adam's lean torso as he slipped his shirt over his head.

"Can I be of any help?" she asked.

"No. Try to go back to sleep." He sat on the bed and attempted to put on his boots.

She got up, came to him, then kneeled on the floor in front of her husband. "Here, let me help."

A moment later, he was donning his coat. His hand on the door knob, he turned back to her. "I'll be right back."

She had just slipped back into their bed when the door to their chamber opened.

"You're certainly back - -." She saw that it wasn't Adam. A strange man with a patch over his left eye stormed into her room.

"You have the wrong room!"

He closed the door behind him and came closer to her. "No I don't, Mrs. Birming'am."

Terror shot through her. Did the man mean to ravish her? She leapt from the bed and backed herself into a corner.

Not the brightest move.

He moved to her. Not tall like Adam, this horrid man was extremely muscular. And menacing. And she did not know how she could protect herself against him. If only she had a weapon.

By the time she remembered Anne Fortescue's brothers' advice about kneeing in the groin, the man with the eye patch had completely backed into the corner with her. She couldn't have placed a book between them. Heartbeat stampeding, she fought him when he tried to tie a large sash around her mouth. He didn't want anyone to hear her scream. Her strength was no match for his. Her cries were successfully muffled.

Good Lord, is he going to kill me? She suddenly remembered about all those mad men Aunt Harriett had told her about in wicked London. She fleetingly thought of the man on the horse who had followed them that day they went to Madame De Guerney's. Had he followed her to Yorkshire?

He lifted her body off the floor and flung her over his shoulders. She tried to scream, but the cloth muffled her sounds. Hadn't Adam said he'd be right back? She prayed he'd come storming through that door and save her.

"I'm getting you out of 'ere right now before yer 'usband   gets   wise   and   comes   back."

$\mathcal{C}$**hapter 17**

Where in the devil was the person who wished to see him? Adam went from one downstairs parlor to another, but each chamber was empty. Had *everyone* gone to bed? What the devil time was it? When he neared the tap room—the last chamber—he heard voices. Not as many as there had been earlier, but at least someone was still awake. There, he would surely find the man responsible for intruding on his sleep.

Interruption of sleep aside, he could not help but to be upset. He thought of his bank as other men thought of their children. It had been his life for the past decade. What could have gone wrong?

One aproned man stood behind the bar; two faced it. All three looked up when he entered the chamber, then they went back to their conversation without acknowledging his presence. That none of them attempted to speak to him told him none of them could be the man who sought him.

He waited for a few moments. When no one tried to approach him, he approached the bar.

"What would you like, sir?" the man behind the bar asked.

"A woman whom I believe works for you awakened me a few minutes ago and told me that a man wished to see me downstairs on a vastly important matter."

The bartender's bushy brows lowered. "Are you certain the woman was one of my staff? No woman has worked 'ere this hour past."

"I'm not really certain. My name's Adam Birmingham. Has anyone been asking for me?"

The man shook his head solemnly. "No one besides these two men has been 'ere in the past 'alf hour."

The other two men nodded in confirmation.

Adam exhaled angrily. What was he to do? His first instinct was to await the man here in the tavern.

But for some reason he could not fathom, he suddenly felt compelled to return to the bedchamber he shared with Emma. Something told him she was in danger. At the thought, he raced from one dark chamber to another, then took the stairs two at a time. His heart raced—*not* from exertion—when he reached the landing.

The door to their bedchamber stood open.

He sped to the chamber, tore through their parlor, and stood facing their bed, sickened.

Emma was gone.

He fought against the optimistic hope that she'd gone looking for him. The dress she'd worn that evening still hung on a wall hook. She would never have left their chamber dressed in her night shift. Even if it weren't such a beastly cold night.

His stomach went queasy. Fury slammed into him. Someone had abducted his wife. Good God Almighty, would she end up as her uncle had? At the thought, a pain as palpable as a sword tore through him. Involuntarily, he wailed.

William! William would know what to do. He sprinted to his brother's chamber and pounded at the door. This was no time to be considerate of others. "Wake up!" he yelled.

William, hiding his nakedness behind the door, yanked it open. "What the hell?"

"Someone's taken Emma!"

Lady Sophia shrieked.

"I'll throw on my clothes." The door closed on Adam.

Nick's door was thrown open. "What the devil's going on?"

Adam moved to him. Nick had put on his breeches but was holding up the flap with his hands. "It's Emma. Someone's abducted her."

"I'll be right there."

A moment later, the three Birmingham brothers, now fully dressed, gathered in the corridor. Lady Sophia, most of her hiding behind the door, poked out her head. "It must have something to do with the man who followed us in London."

Adam felt as if he could lose the contents of his stomach. "What man? You knew my wife was in danger?"

"I'm sorry," she said in a shaky voice.

"What did he look like?" Adam demanded.

"We didn't see him. My coachman told us a lone man on a horse had followed us from your house to Madame De Guerney's."

Adam winced. "Dear God."

"Quick!" William said. "We can arm ourselves from the stash beneath my coach seats. I'll have Thompson come."

William's valet was far more than a valet. He was the kind of man one wanted fighting on one's side.

While they waited for their horses to be

harnessed, Adam asked the sleepy groom if he saw a man carrying a woman.

"Indeed I did! When I 'eard the 'orse's hooves pounding away so quickly, I feared someone had stolen one of ours. I looked from me window. I couldn't see real good, but it was most peculiar to see a woman with such a little bit of clothing on such a cold night. And I coulda swore there was somethin' tied around 'er mouth."

Adam's voice was splintered when he asked, "Which road did they take?" Poor little Emma. She might die from the elements—if not at the hands of the cut-throat.

"They went south."

"Back to London," William murmured.

Adam was harnessing his own horse. He had to leave immediately—before something unspeakable happened to his wife. Just imagining how cold she must be made him feel as if he could weep like a woman.

But this wasn't the time for weeping. It was the time for action. Cursing, he mounted and sped off, a sword at his side, a knife sheathed on his leg, and a musket fastened to his saddle.

His brothers and William's valet—all bruising riders—soon caught up with him.

* * *

The horrid man who had abducted her had slung Emma over his horse as if she were a rolled-up rug. The blood rushed to her head. There was no way she could remove the cloth which silenced her because her hands were bound behind her with hemp.

Even if it meant falling on her head, she was willing to propel herself onto the ground in order to get away from him. Once on the ground, though, success was not guaranteed, given her inability to scream.

Before she could shimmy her midsection off the horse, her abductor mounted and spurred on the horse at a prodigious clip. To leap from the horse at that rate of speed would be suicide.

She had initially been so frozen by fear that she hadn't even thought of her physical misery. But as they raced through the frigid night air, she became sickeningly aware of how brutally cold she was. Her teeth chattered. She felt as if the chill had penetrated into her bones. Her skin was in danger of frostbite. She had never known such discomfort. She might even die of exposure.

Which was preferable to being violated by this odious man. It did seem odd to her that if he wanted to ravish her, why was he not doing so within minutes of leaving the inn?

A chilling thought obliterated everything else. Perhaps defilement was not his intent. Perhaps her abduction was tied to her uncle's murder. Perhaps Ashburnham meant to kill the woman who was standing in the way of his ill-gotten gains.

Fear paralyzed her.

If her mouth weren't bound she could have asked the man with the eye patch where he was taking her. She could have asked him how much he was being paid. Surely Adam would pay him more for her safe release. She was certain of it. What a pity she was unable to talk to the disgusting man.

Was he a killer? Had he been told to kill her?

Tears came when she thought of dying so young. If only she had been able to capture Adam's heart before she died. If only she could have found herself in his protective arms.

As their overloaded horse slowed its gait and her whole body began to tremble violently from the bitter cold, she fantasized about being back in the bed she had shared with Adam. How secure she had felt, how utterly content she had been. If only she could see him one last time. If only she could tell him how much she had come to love him.

Even if he could never love her as he loved Maria, she knew in her heart that in some small way he did love her. He would be sad at her death.

Now she wept. For her and Adam.

* * *

His horse pounding through the barren countryside beneath a moon obscured by heavy clouds, Adam felt guilty that he wore a greatcoat while his unfortunate wife had not even the warmth of a woolen dress. He prayed he would get to her before . . . before someone harmed her, before she perished from exposure to the cold.

Not long after he left the inn's livery stable, his brothers and William's valet caught up with him. He prayed the four heavily armed men would be able to overpower Emma's abductor. He prayed that the vile man would take pity on his petite victim and cover her exposed body. He prayed they would not be too late to save her.

The Birmingham brothers had always been able to count on one another in a crisis. Tonight, though, his brothers raced with the same abandon as he. It was as if each of them reacted as they would have, had their own cherished wives been in the same danger Emma was. His chest constricted. Having just begun to feel a deepening connection with his own wife, he felt all the sicker over losing her, felt all the sicker that he'd not been a true husband to her. How he wished he had taken her into his arms last night and made her his wife in the purest sense.

He would give all his tomorrows to have that one night back.

It ripped his heart to recall her telling him that he was her dearest friend. Now he wished he could tell her she was and always would be his dearest friend. He couldn't lose her—not now, now that he realized how very dear she was to him.

Now that her very existence was threatened, he fondly recalled the many pleasant hours they had spent together. He hadn't enjoyed anything so much since he'd been a cricket-mad lad who had hated to see the sun come down at night. Every moment with Emma had been even more pleasurable.

He regretted that he'd said his farewells to her each night at her bedchamber door. *Why did I not try to be the husband of her heart?*

It only now occurred to him that his young wife was the wife of *his* heart.

Rage tore through him when he thought of that man hurting her. Adam would kill him with no compunction. The idea of Emma being murdered made Adam feel as if his own heart had abruptly stopped beating.

Adam wished like the devil he knew how much time had lapsed between her abduction and the moment he set off on his horse. It had to be nearly twenty minutes. He drew a deep breath. Twenty minutes' head start which he had to make up. It might take a few hours to do so, but his horse had to be considerably quicker than one driven by a man hindered by carrying a woman. Even if she was small.

* * *

All Adam cared about was getting his wife safe and warm. He knew he could count on William to do whatever it took to subdue Emma's abductor.

If they caught up with them. He had no assurances she was even on this road. What if the man had taken her to a house . . . for vile purposes? Adam's blood ran cold at the thought.

Turning his thoughts in a more hopeful direction, he believed if they were on this road Emma and her abductor couldn't possibly be traveling as fast as he and his brothers. So why in the devil hadn't they gained on them by now?

He was getting discouraged, but when he saw a lone horse on the distant horizon, his pulse spiked. He rode faster. He soon knew with sickening certainty he'd found his wife.

When they got close enough for him to see the way she was slung over the horse, he thought she was dead. It was as if every organ in his body instantly shut down. Overwhelming grief numbed him.

Then he saw her head twist around as if she were trying to glimpse at their followers. *Thank God.*

He was bombarded with murderous thoughts at how inhumanly she had been treated. Her arms and legs were bare—in this bitter cold. As he drew nearer he saw that her slim hands were tied behind her back. If the fiend had bound her hands, why in the hell did he not allow her sit the horse? She could hardly have gotten away.

And why in the hell hadn't the cur had enough compassion to at least offer her a blanket?

Adam longed to turn the tables on the vicious

man. Would he like to be stripped almost bare and forced to ride through a frigid night with the blood rushing to his head?

That they were able to catch up with the vile man brought joy on several levels—first and most critical, Emma was alive. And the man must not have defiled her innocence.

When they got close enough, William yelled out for the man to stop.

Without even turning back to look at them, the abductor merely dug his heels into his poor beast's flanks. He had no intentions of either stopping or of giving her up.

William was not deterred. Once more he yelled for the man to stop. This time he added, "If you don't stop, you'll be killed."

Adam was startled. As complete as his own hatred was toward this man who had so abused his wife, he did not want him killed. They needed him. Adam was almost certain Ashburnham had ordered Emma's abduction, and they needed proof of that man's depravity.

William was likely trying to scare the man. Adam must defer to William in this situation. William had vast experience dealing with unscrupulous men. Ashburnham was the only unscrupulous man Adam had ever met face to face.

William's actions were so quick, Adam had no time to react. William's hand slid to the sheath in his boot and in one fluid move hurled a silvery knife toward the man's shoulder.

Adam exhaled. William only meant to disable the man—not kill him.

The man cursed. William's plan must have worked because the man started to release

Emma.

Adam raced to the side where her head dangled. He meant to catch her before she was slung to the ground.

Then a peculiar thing happened. The horse stopped.

The man who'd terrorized Adam's wife slumped and fell to the ground.

"Emma," Adam said, "I'm here. Allow me to get you." He dismounted and lifted her away. When he saw the blood on her dress, he panicked.

Then he realized it was her abductor's blood.

He needed to get her warm. He needed to cut the rope from her wrists. But at this moment what he needed most was to take her little body in his arms and hold her.

$\mathcal{C}$hapter 18

The temperatures neared freezing and the night's darkness had not fully lifted, but for a brief moment Emma felt as if she were in a sunny field of summer wildflowers. That's how being held in Adam's arms made her feel. That and so much more. Elation. Relief. Security. And overwhelming love.

She could almost forget her wretched discomfort.

She need not worry for herself, not when Adam was there. He was so supremely good at taking care of her.

He stood her up and stepped back, his gaze utterly solemn when their eyes met. Without saying a word, he removed his own huge coat and placed it over her shoulders. It came past her bare feet and dragged on the ground.

"I can't take your coat," she protested. She felt badly, too, that because of her, his coat was dirtied.

"You will." He helped her put it on and began to fasten it.

"But you'll freeze."

"You're the one who's exposed," he said gruffly. "Your teeth are chattering, and your skin's icy."

The coat felt so good. She was far too cold to argue.

He lifted her into his arms and attempted to tuck the coat around her chilled feet. "I wish I could offer you a warm fire."

"I do, too."

Though the coat helped—as did being so close to him—it would take far more than that before she could completely thaw. Now that she was less uncomfortable, she thought to see what was going on with that odious man with the eye patch.

She turned her head. At first all she saw was Nick towering over the other two men. William was on one knee, and her abductor was lying on the ground.

"My God, I think he's dead," William said. "I only meant to slow him, make him give Emma up. My knife struck his shoulder. That shouldn't be a mortal wound."

Nick shook his head slowly. "Unless he's a bleeder."

Huge amounts of blood oozed from the fallen man and pooled on the ground.

Throughout the nearly unbearable hours in the man's captivity, Emma had (most uncharitably) thought of how much she hated him, how much she wished something terrible would befall him. But she took no consolation now that something terrible *had* taken his life.

Adam cursed. "Now we'll never know for sure who the cur was working for, though God knows, he deserved to die."

Her insides sank. She hadn't thought of that.

"I don't know what you fellows plan to do now," Adam said, "but I need to get my wife somewhere warm. Are we not almost back at Wickley Glen?"

Will nodded. "We can't be more than two miles from it."

"Here, let me help you mount," Nick said.

Adam returned to his horse and handed her to Nick while he mounted, then Nick hoisted her onto the saddle. "She certainly is light!"

Emma wished she weren't so small. Men had a tendency to treat her like a child, and she wanted to be treated like a woman. A married woman.

"I'll need one of you to come with me," Adam said. "I can't very well carry her in like this. Someone will have to bespeak our room."

"I'll come," Nick said. "William will instruct his man on the disposition of this blackguard's body."

The three of them rode no more than ten minutes when they saw the clusters of houses signifying a town.

Nick had to awaken the innkeeper when they reached the King's Arms but he made it well worth the man's inconvenience. He requested the best available accommodations and asked that hot chocolate be brought up to the chamber for his *wife* immediately.

He came back outside to give Adam the key. "Everyone thinks we're twins anyway, so I said I was you. You're in Room 1, the first one at the top of the stairs. They're building a fire as we speak, and I've requested a pot of hot chocolate."

"You have paid?" Adam asked.

"Handsomely. You'll be treated like royalty."

That would be nothing new, Emma thought. The Birminghams were always treated like royalty.

Adam handed her to Nick, then dismounted and once more drew her into his arms. At least, she thought, there was one consolation for possessing very cold feet on a very cold night—and a very good consolation it was.

"I suppose we'll miss your electioneering,"

Adam said.

"Yes, but you won't miss seeing Verity's babe—and Mama won't let you get away without allowing her to meet your wife." Nick smiled at Emma. "I'll send William's coach back for you—with all your clothing. You ought to make Stenson Keyes by late afternoon."

"Why don't you go back with your brother?" she said to Adam. "I'll be fine."

Adam regarded her through narrowed eyes. "Right now, I don't know how I can ever again leave you."

His words were more welcome than an eiderdown quilt.

"I would feel the same if it were Fiona," Nick added, flicking his glance to the inn's door. "When you enter, you can go either left or right. If you go right, you'll find the staircase. It's pretty dark, so be careful carrying her up the stairs."

"Once I'm inside," Emma said, "I can walk."

Nick gave her a pitying gaze. "I wish I could have ordered you some woolen socks."

Adam glared. "Are you not the one who always says anything can be had if one's pockets are deep enough?"

Nick shrugged and began to mount his horse.

After entering the inn, Adam did set her down, then led the way upstairs, holding her hand as they climbed. The door to their chamber was open, and a youthful charwoman was completing her task. She looked at them. "Yer chambers will be warm as toast in no time."

Adam pulled a guinea from his pocket. "There's a guinea for you if you can find a pair of woolen socks for my wife."

"I'll be right back up, sir. Me mum knits them

for everybody in our family. We got our own sheep, you see."

After she left, Adam pulled the parlor's settee in front of the fire, then from the adjacent bedchamber brought a heavy quilt. "Sit here in front of the fire. I'll help wrap this around you." After he covered her, he removed his own gloves and placed them on her icy hands. "I know they're so big you could put both your hands in one."

She giggled. Funny, an hour ago she thought she would never giggle again.

Though the chamber was still not warm, it was a thousand times better than what she'd experienced throughout the night.

Adam came to sit near her on the settee. "I'm so very sorry for what you've had to endure tonight. Other than his complete disregard for your comfort, did that man hurt you?"

She shook her head. "I thought he must mean to ravish me, but apparently that was not his intent."

"Good. Did he say anything, anything at all that gave a clue about what his intentions were? Did he say he was taking you to someone?"

"Like Ashburnham?"

"Then you've made the same deduction I have."

She nodded. "It wasn't long before I realized we were covering the same route we'd come, so I suspected his destination was London, but even before that I had guessed it was Ashburnham's scheme."

"He didn't say anything?"

"Nothing. I suppose if my mouth had not been bound, there could have been some dialogue. I most certainly would have told him my husband would pay him more than Ashburnham."

"I would have given him anything to secure your safe release." His voice was oddly gentle, almost as if he were choking back tender emotions.

Every second of discomfort she'd experienced was worth this moment. How cherished she felt, knowing he would give his fortune to save her life. How cozy she felt, being in this intimate setting with the man she adored.

The charwoman—or was it a char girl?—returned, a huge gap-toothed smile on her face, as she presented Adam a pair of gray stockings. "These be brand new," she said with pride.

"They're lovely, and we're most grateful to you." He handed her a guinea.

Adam sat on the far end of the settee, uncovered Emma's feet, and began to place the stockings on her. "God, you feel like ice!"

"I'm sure I'll be warm soon. The fire's going strong now. "

Her breath came in staggering gusts. She was nearly unraveled from the intimacy of him slowly putting on the stockings, smoothing them up her ankles, then along her calves. It would have been embarrassing except for the fact he was her husband.

After both stockings were on, he cradled one foot within his big hands and began to massage it. "I'm very concerned about you."

She sighed. "I'm like a stray pup you've taken into your care."

"I used to think that way about you," he said with little laugh. He looked her in the eye, his gaze intense. "Not anymore. Somehow, I have come to think of you as my wife."

Her heartbeat pounded. In a good way. Their

eyes still locked. "Since that day at St. George's," she said in a thin voice, "the only way I've thought of you is as my husband."

He lifted a brow. "And I thought you thought of me as your best friend."

Their eyes held. "I am told that in the best marriages, one's spouse *is* one's best friend."

"So my brothers say." He swallowed. It was as if what he was going to say next was difficult. "I . . . have come to think of you as my dearest friend." His hands massaged her feet even more tenderly in small, excruciatingly gentle circles. He tucked that foot back beneath the quilt, drew out the other one and began to massage it.

He drew a deep breath. "After you were taken I was sorry I hadn't told you I thought of you as my best friend." Now his voice cracked. "I feared I'd never get to tell you."

She couldn't believe this was happening to her. Her husband was being so . . . well, close to romantic. She'd always known he genuinely cared for her, but she was ecstatic to learn the object of his affections had transitioned from puppy dog to wife.

Theirs was going to be a true marriage! He would still need time to adjust his thinking, but she was more than willing to wait. Even it took a lifetime. She could think of no one with whom she'd rather spend the rest of her life.

What had been the worst night of her life had resulted in the happiest moment of her life. It had been worth every second of misery.

How many times since she and Adam had married had she thought *This is the happiest moment in my life?* Nearly every day with him had been more pleasurable than the one before it. She certainly could not expect the rest of her life to continue in escalating happiness.

Why was it her happiest moments had been preceded by vile occurrences? Of course, had it not been for the vile murder of Uncle Simon, she never would have met Adam, never would have wed him, never would have known what it was like to love someone as madly as she loved her husband.

She reached out to touch his hand. "You've made me very happy."

Neither spoke after that. She understood that it had not been easy for him to speak of his emotions. Apparently he had to be deep in his cups to do that. He had said enough to nearly wipe from her memory the hardships she'd endured that night.

After he finished massaging her feet, he turned his attentions to her raw wrists. He started to curse when he saw the oozing red skin there, then stopped himself. "I will not swear in front of a lady, but at this moment I'm happy the man who did this to you is dead."

"I wished him dead, but now I wish he'd only been maimed. For William's sake."

Adam nodded. "My brother will take it hard that he's responsible for another man's death." His gaze dropped to her reddened wrists. "Does it hurt badly?"

"Only when I think about it." She shrugged. "Don't trouble yourself. Only time will heal such wounds."

"I wish there were something I could do to ease the pain."

Without artifice, she slapped on a bright countenance. "Then you should continue saying those wonderful things to me. I don't think about my discomfort when you do."

An amused expression on his face, he asked, "And to what wonderful things would you be referring?"

"Being best friends . . . worrying about never seeing me again . . . and most especially, I loved it when you said you didn't know how you could ever leave me again."

He threw his head back and roared with laughter. "My dear one must be making a remarkable recovery." His face went serious. "And for that I am exceedingly grateful."

He reached across the expanse of the settee and cradled her face. "You've not slept all night. Please, my dear wife, you need to try to sleep."

"You didn't sleep, either."

"If you promise to sleep, I will."

* * *

The grueling night had left his wife exhausted. Within seconds of her closing her eyes, she was in a deep slumber. As tired as he was, he could not sleep. The rational side of him told him no one would storm into this quiet bedchamber and harm his wife. But the events of the previous night had robbed him of rational thought. He was still governed by the paralyzing fear he'd felt when he realized someone had taken Emma. He still blamed himself for leaving her, still was terrified the mortifying event would be repeated.

He could not allow himself to close his eyes—not until he had his precious wife back on well-guarded Birmingham property, property that would become even more well guarded. The Birminghams did, after all, employ their own well-trained, well-equipped army.

All he could think of was protecting Emma. For now, he meant it when he'd said he would not leave her side. Nothing, absolutely nothing, could persuade him to abandon her even for a moment.

He kept the candle burning so he could watch her pretty face as she slept. The words that had passed between them here in this room were some of the most welcome he'd ever heard. He kept recalling her sweet voice when she'd said, "Since that day at St. George's I've never thought of you as anything but my husband."

Her words had a similar effect to his horse winning the Derby. Such sheer elation!

Even besieged with worry for her, just sitting before the fire so close to Emma filled him with contentment. He had a few hours to reflect on this marriage, something he'd not consciously done before. Those initial feelings that he'd been cheated of a loving marriage vanished like the morning dew. He'd not truly wanted this marriage, but now he could not think of life without Emma. Last night had taught him how very dear she was to him.

He realized now how empty his life was before Emma. Yes, he'd had something with Maria, but that something was only physical. Her beauty stroked his ego amongst men of rank. He was ashamed now that such a thing had once been important to him.

If he could turn back the clocks of time to when he was unmarried, and if he were given the choice between taking Maria or Emma for his wife, he would not hesitate for even a second. Emma was the woman with whom he wanted to spend the rest of his life.

He thought about Nick's and Will's solid

marriages and realized he *had* always craved a loving partnership like theirs. Deep inside, he'd craved a wife who would also be his best friend.

In Emma, he would have that. The realization made him feel complete.

There was just one aspect of their marriage that was lacking. One very important aspect. How hard it had been for him earlier that night not to draw her into his arms, kiss her with pent-up passions, and carry her to *their* bed.

After the ordeal of her night, he would never have put his carnal needs above her comfort. It had, though, been beastly hard not to make love to her when she looked at him as lovingly as she did, especially when she alluded to her affection for him.

He thought perhaps—after she was out of danger—theirs could become a complete marriage. The very idea aroused him.

He believed she was not averse to being his wife in every way.

But that last, final step to the completion of their marriage could not be taken quickly in a posting inn. Nor could it be stolen because of his acute desire for her.

He planned to court his wife.

$\mathcal{C}$hapter 19

He'd thought to initiate his courting by stealing kisses throughout the journey back to Stenson Keyes but Lady Sophia foiled his scheme. She had insisted on comforting her "dear sister" after the harrowing experience of the previous night.

Her intrusion into their little mobile love nest put Adam out of sorts. Instead of the intimate sweet talk and nibbly kisses between his wife and him, he was being subjected to Lady Sophia's overly dramatic tirade against the man who snatched Emma from her bedchamber. "It's a very good thing the vile creature has died after his abominable treatment of you! Tell me, my dear sister, were you not terrified when he stole you from your bed?"

"Indeed I was."

"I daresay, it was the most frightening thing that could happen. Did you think he might kill you?"

"It certainly crossed my mind."

"I was thinking," Lady Sophia mused aloud, "that since he was a lone man on a horse . . . do you suppose he may have been the very same man who followed us to Madame De Guerney's that day?"

Emma's gaze flashed to him. "Adam and I think there may be a possible connection between last night's abduction and my uncle's murder."

Lady Sophia shrieked. "How horrifying!"

"The abductor was not the man we suspect, but we believe he may be working for him," Adam said.

Lady Sophia's brows lowered. "Then he was bringing you to London so that awful man could kill you?"

"If we are right in our assumptions," Emma said, "I'm sure he planned to kill me—but not until he learned if I'd shared my suspicions with others."

"I am just so utterly relieved that you're not seriously hurt." Lady Sophia's gaze dropped to the raw circles around Emma's wrists. "And I will admit I had feared that the awful man might have . . . tried to take liberties with you. I suppose that's why I had to come. I wanted to comfort you."

"I'm deeply appreciative of your concern."

Adam hated this talk of Emma's wretched night. He wanted to block it from his memory, though he never wanted to let down his guard again, not when it concerned his wife's safety.

Last night could have been worse. Much worse. He let out a silent prayer of thanks that Emma was safe, that her innocence had not been compromised, that she had suffered no serious injuries.

In spite of his resentment of her presence, Adam, too, was grateful that Lady Sophia had so thoroughly welcomed his wife into the family. Before his siblings had married into the nobility, he'd never really trusted those of high rank. But the Earl of Agar and his sister, along with Lady Sophia, whose family was one of the oldest in the kingdom, could not have been kinder to him and his kinsmen.

Adam smiled when he thought of how dearly Lord Agar cherished their sister Verity. Someone possessed of a nature as sweet as Verity's deserved a happy marriage.

**

That afternoon he saw the Agars, along with his infant nephew, the heir to the Agar earldom. He was thankful neither they nor his mother referred to the wretched incident that had caused his and his wife's delay. He didn't want anything to detract from this moment when he could proudly introduce his wife to the rest of his family.

As he strolled toward Verity, holding his wife's hand and eyeing the babe in his sister's arms, he said, "It seems we each have new members of the family to introduce."

Verity's happy gaze moved to Emma, but she spoke to Adam. "You first." Her feminine voice trilled with delight.

"My dearest sister . . ." he bowed ever so slightly and gave a mock cough, "Lady Agar, my I present to you my wife, Emma?"

Emma dropped into a curtsey but did not speak until Verity addressed her.

Verity's eyes, so much like his own, shimmered as she regarded Emma. "How happy we all are that Adam now has a wife of his own, and how happy we are to meet you."

That was an exceedingly long sentence for shy Verity. Perhaps being a countess was building her confidence. She'd always exuded poise—remarkable, given that she was raised among three rowdy lads.

"I am so excited to finally meet you! You're a

beautiful version of the man I adore most on earth."

He felt as if he'd just grown a foot. He was so proud of Emma, so delighted over her unfailing exuberance, and incredibly touched over the way in which she had referred to him. *The man I adore most on earth.*

Was she sincere? Or was she merely playing the role of a smitten bride? Knowing Emma, he could not imagine her speaking anything but the truth. Her youthful excitement must be contagious. He felt as if he were soaring.

"And now," Verity said, pride in her voice as she gazed adoringly at the babe in her arms, "I should like to present to you the Viscount Duckworth."

Adam refrained from the urge to call the heir Duckie—the name his father bore back at Eton.

Emma rushed to nearly smash her face into the babe's. "What perfection! Pray, don't be offended if I say he's beautiful."

Verity's lashes lowered, and she spoke softly. "I think so, too. And so does Randy."

"Please," Emma said, "may I hold him?"

Verity smiled and handed him over. "Of course."

Adam wouldn't have wanted to hold anything that tiny. How in the devil did Agar father such a small little thing?

"Oh look, my dearest," Emma said to him, "how precious he is!"

He came to stand beside his wife, and he was nearly overwhelmed with tender feelings. For a brief second, he wished Emma were holding his son, wished theirs was the loving family that Agar's and Verity's was.

It was difficult to tell if the babe looked like the

Agars or the Birminghams. His hair—what little there was of it—was decidedly dark like Verity's. He couldn't tell what color the little fellow's eyes were because he continued to sleep, even with all the noise that surrounded him.

"I don't think little Duckworth looks like anyone in either family," he declared.

Verity let out a little laugh. "You are unaccustomed to babes. He does possess the Agar nose, and we're told he will have the Birmingham height."

Adam's mouth formed an o. "But he's so short!"

Both Emma and Verity laughed.

"He's only a month old!" Emma said.

How comfortable Emma looked with a babe in her arms. A natural mother. He could never again think of her as a girl. His chest constricted.

"He is fine lad, is me first grandson."

Adam whirled around to face his mother. To his surprise, she clutched the hand of Nick's little natural daughter, Emmie. He'd never before heard his mother boast. Being a grandmother must have mellowed the stern woman. He kissed her on the cheek. "Mother, I should like you to meet my wife, Emma."

His mother's gaze swept over her, and she nodded approvingly. He wished she would have said something to her newest daughter-in-law, but his mother lacked social graces.

Emma was not be deterred. "It is such a longed-for pleasure to meet the woman who raised three such fine sons. You must be the best mother in all of England—for Adam is certainly the best man I've ever known."

Of course, his sheltered wife knew few men. He almost erupted into laughter over Emma's frequent use of hyperbole. He supposed it was one of the things that had endeared her to him. Each day for her was always *the best* ever. Would that she could make such a statement for the rest of her days.

At the idea that they'd be together for the rest of their days, something inside him glowed.

"Methinks Adam's new wife is prone to exaggeration," his mother said to Emma. His insides sank. Was Mama going to chide his well-meaning wife? Then she continued. "But it's kind of you to say those things." She held out her arms. "May I hold my little angle?"

Emma handed over Verity's babe. Little Emmie stood on her tiptoes to stroke little Randolph's hair.

Did his mother ever refer to her own children as *little angels*? Never. What the devil had come over her?

Emma was eyeing Nick's child. "This must be Emmie! I have so wanted to meet the little girl who shares my name."

The child looked up and met Emma's affectionate gaze, and shy smile eased across her little face. "You're Emmie, too?"

Emma dropped to her knees. "Not exactly. I'm Emma. No one ever called me Emmie, though I would have loved it. That's the kind of name given by someone who loves a child very much."

"My papa's the one who called me that."

Nick was besotted over the child—as the child was besotted over her father. Lady Fiona had won the admiration of everyone in their family with her deep affection for Nick's natural daughter. Lady Fiona had been the first member of the nobility to earn Adam's complete admiration. Then her brother's devotion to Verity convinced him that not all aristocrats were insensitive elitists. Lady Sophia, too, was a great favorite with every member of the Birmingham family.

"And how do you like your Aunt Verity's babe?"

"I love him very much. Auntie allowed me to hold him—as long as I was sitting down."

"Come, little poppet, and I'll let ye hold him again," her grandmother said. Glancing up at Emma, she said, "'Tis been a pleasure to meet you, Emma."

Emma stepped closer and pressed her lips to little Randolph's cheek, then to her mother-in-law's. "The pleasure's mine. I'm so happy to be a part of your family."

Adam moved to his wife and draped his arm around her shoulders. "My wife was an only child."

"I feel sorry for only children," his mother said, looking down at Emmie, who clung to her skirts. "Emmie needs brothers and sisters."

Emmie's eyes widened. "I should love to have a sister, or even a brother."

Smiling broadly, Adam shook his head. "Methinks my mother has grown exceedingly fond of being a grandmother."

"So I have." She walked off.

* * *

In the same large inn where Emma had been abducted, the entire family gathered that night to share a meal at one long trestle table that ran parallel to the chamber's tall brick fireplace. There was so much warmth in the room, Emma could no longer recall the feel of her icy limbs the previous night.

Lord Agar favorably impressed Emma, largely

due to the tenderness his wife evoked in him. Even though he was born to enormous rank, Lord Agar had much in common with the sons of an uncouth businessman. They were all devoted husbands.

Emma detected a faint resemblance between Lady Fiona and her brother, but it surprised her that he was not nearly as handsome as the Birmingham brothers. Because Lady Fiona was so lovely, Emma had expected Lord Agar's appearance to be considerably above normal.

"Where is Mother?" Emma asked. It was the first time in her life she'd addressed a woman as *mother,* and she rather liked the idea of it, even though Adam's mother had not been overwhelmingly friendly to her. She took no offense because Adam had stressed that his mother's lack of warmth was only equaled by her lack of manners.

"She refused to allow us to bring little Randolph's nurse," Verity said. "She adores taking care of him—with *help* from Emmie!"

"Our daughter is baby mad," Lady Fiona said.

How touching that Lady Fiona thought of Nick's little daughter as her own.

"Mother may never return to Great Acres," Adam quipped.

Lady Sophia shook her head. "I believe you're wrong. Once Lady Fiona or I—or Emma—has a child, your mother will rush back down south. She's as baby mad as little Emmie."

Emma bubbled inside at the thought of having Adam's babe.

Adam eyed Nick. "Has it occurred to you that another person, a benevolent woman, has taken possession of our mother?"

They all burst out laughing.

William and Nick both nodded.

"How did the electioneering go?" Adam asked.

Lady Fiona's gentle expression turned to excitement. "Oh, you should have heard Nick! He was magnificent."

Though every woman at the table was madly in love with her husband, Emma believed Lady Fiona's adoration of Nick topped all of them.

William nodded. "I think everyone was impressed."

"Indeed," Lord Agar added. "Lord Petersham said Nick could speak to the people better than anyone he's ever heard." He eyed his sister. "And without sounding too much of a braggart, I must say my sister was perfectly charming. After the speech when everyone began to mingle about the assembly rooms, she personally served punch to every man in line and was most impressive, asking each man about his family."

"Yes, I think half the men in the room fell in love with her," William said.

"You all are making me blush," Lady Fiona said. (Though Emma saw not a particle of blush on that lady's creamy face.)

His dark eyes shimmering with love, Nick met his wife's gaze. "And you blush most beautifully, my love."

"You must not forget how gracious Verity was," Lady Fiona said. "She's the one who knew nearly every man by name."

Lord Agar beamed. "I am always proud of my wife."

Unlike Lady Fiona, who only spoke of blushing, Verity actually did blush.

Emma could sigh. Just being surrounded by so

much love made her happy. Perhaps her delight was somewhat coloured by her own husband's affectionate attentions throughout the day.

Emma eyed Lord Agar. "So it's looking as if Nick will win?"

"I believe so," Lord Agar said.

Nick held up a hand. "You all are over confident. My opponent is highly qualified."

Lady Fiona pouted. "He doesn't hold a candle to you!"

"Spoken like a loving wife," Nick said, reaching to stoke her cheek affectionately.

Lord Agar went to rise. "I hate that we must leave. We had tried this morning to procure rooms here, but the inn is full, likely of Birminghams! We've got a two-hour drive which won't put us home until after midnight."

Verity looked at Emma. "I would have ridden all day to meet my dear new sister."

Emma was overwhelmed. "I feel the same. I'd even have ridden a whole week."

"But," Adam added, "my wife has the misfortune of being married to a man who cannot take much time away from his business."

"Then I'm very happy I married a man who does not have to work," Verity said, looking up adoringly at her husband.

Emma tried looking adoringly at Adam. "I could never actually travel without you—especially for weeks at time."

"After last night, I'll never let you!"

Having someone care for her so openly thrilled her. She had known that Aunt Harriett loved her, but her aunt had never shown it, never spoken of it.

Emma loved being part of the Birmingham

family

* * *

Adam would allow Emma an appropriate period of time in which to ready for bed. It would be best if she were asleep when he came to their chamber so he wouldn't be tempted by the provocative effect she had upon him as of late. It might be better, but it was not what he really wanted. His breath grew ragged when he thought of watching her face brighten when he entered the chamber, of seeing the trace of her nipples beneath the fine lawn of the night shift, of climbing into their bed.

After he walked her to their chamber—he wasn't taking any chances that a threat lurked in either the hallway or in their rooms—and saw her safely locked inside, William drew him aside and spoke in a low voice. "Nick and I need to talk to you."

He followed his brother to a small, dimly lit parlor where Nick awaited them, three fresh bumpers of ale standing on the rough wooden table, a fire burning in a corner of the chamber.

Once they were seated, William began. "We wanted to speak to you about this business with the murderer of Emma's uncle. Who is the fellow?"

"We believe it's the clerk who worked at the Ceylon Tea Company under Simon Hastings, a man named Ashburnham. We have fairly substantial proof that he forged Hastings' newest will, and we strongly suspect that he murdered Hastings with poison." He filled them in on all the details he and Emma had culled over a several-day period.

"I suppose it's occurred to you that Ashburnham may be behind Emma's abduction,"

Nick said.

"Yes. Emma and I both think that's likely the case."

William's eyes narrowed. "It's got to terrify you to know that they must have meant to kill your wife once this Ashburnham found out what he needed to know."

Adam felt as if a cannon ball plunged into his gut. "It does terrify me."

"You and Emma can't go on indefinitely living in such fear. You can't guard her every minute of every day," Nick said.

"We have the best trained, best armed men in the kingdom in our employ," Adam countered.

Nick frowned. "That's hardly fair to Emma, having her constantly followed by heavily armed men."

"Nick and I have been discussing it, and we think you need to bring out this Ashburnham."

Adam leaned back and regarded his brothers as if they'd just sprouted horns. "How do you propose that I do that?"

"You set a trap," William said.

Adam thought on it for a moment. "I can't think of any way to do that without jeopardizing my wife."

William's face was inscrutable. "The only way it will work *is* for you to use Emma as bait."

Anger surged through Adam. "Absolutely not!"

Nick held up a hand. "Hear us out."

"We would never put her in danger," William continued. "You—as well as our most highly qualified soldiers—will discreetly follow her at all times. We'll merely make it *appear* that's she traveling about the city alone."

Adam stood, his fists coiled. "Nothing can

persuade me to put my wife in danger. Again." He stormed from the chamber.

By the time he reached their bedchamber, Emma was fast asleep.

$\mathcal{C}$hapter 20

Across the carriage, William's and Lady Sophia's thighs touched, and their fingers intertwined. Such marital bliss could convert the most confirmed bachelor.

Adam moved across the coach seat until he felt the warmth of Emma's legs against his. Her pressed both his hands around hers. Just getting a wisp of a whiff of his wife's rose scent reinforced Adam's new-found contentment with marriage. There was nowhere on earth he'd rather be than in this coach at this moment with this woman.

He was grateful they had been spared rain. Any delay would push them back another day on the road, an additional day away from his bank. He stopped his line of thought. The bank was no longer the most important thing in his life. Until he'd married, his business had been his life. Now, Emma was. He couldn't return to the bank until he knew she was safe.

They had left Stenson Keyes at dawn and driven beneath blue skies through pleasant countryside, with short stops along with way. He felt sorry for those who rode in the mail coaches that sped from one town to another with no concern for their passengers' comfort.

"Did you ride the mail coach to London?" he asked his wife.

"Indeed I did. It was the first time I'd ever ridden any distance to speak of in a coach, and I must say it did *not* compare favorably to riding in a Birmingham coach."

"Then it was an unpleasant experience for you?" he asked.

She shrugged. "I suppose it could have been unpleasant had I not been so exceedingly excited. Coming to London was the great adventure of my life. Nothing could have marred my happiness."

"Pray, Emma," Lady Sophia said, "what was the worst part about your journey in a mail coach?"

Emma giggled. "The fat man who sat next to me."

Lady Sophia also giggled. "Let us hope he was at least tidy."

"Not at all," Emma said with a slow shake of her head. "I could not determine if he smelled of rancid hog's pudding or of the labors of hard work such as . . ." She faced her husband, an amused smile lighting her face, "chopping wood."

Now Adam burst out laughing over their own private jest. "My wife ridicules me because I've never taken an axe to a log."

Lady Sophia turned to her husband. "Have you?"

"Does breaking down a door with an axe count?"

"No," his wife answered.

Emma's eyes widened as she peered at William. "When, pray tell, did you ever have to break down a door with an axe?"

"You did not know my husband used to offer his . . . services to the Foreign Office?"

"I didn't."

Lady Sophia shrugged. "I didn't either until

after we were married."

William shrugged. "I'm hopelessly tamed now. I was issued an ultimatum. It was either my beautiful Isadore or my clandestine activities."

"I understand how Lady Sophia must have felt." A flicker of admiration in her eyes, Emma looked at William. "Your clandestine activities, though, sound extraordinarily exciting."

Lady Sophia glared. "There is nothing exciting about having people wanting to kill you."

"I do understand that," Emma said in a low voice, squeezing Adam's hand.

The solemnity of her words made them think of her own brush with men who wanted her dead. None of their party spoke for a few moments.

"Allow me to ask you this," Emma finally said, a pleasant lilt to her voice, "have any of *you* ever ridden in a mail coach?"

Each said, "No."

A while later, Emma said, "I do feel wretched that Lady Sophia, Adam, and I couldn't be in Stenson Keyes to support Nick."

"It's like the entire journey and the terrible experiences we endured were all for naught," Adam said.

"Oh, but they weren't *all* terrible experiences," his wife said. "Except for that one night, I've had so much fun." She sighed. "I suppose it's the most fun I've ever had."

Everyone in the coach smiled at her.

"My wife has not only led a dull life, but she's also given to speak in hyperbole." Adam smiled down at her.

"Emma's cheerful countenance is one of the things that makes her so charming."

Charming. Yes, that word *did* suit his wife.

"Thank you." Emma's voice almost squeaked.

"I'm very thankful you two have been so kind to my wife."

Emma started to yawn, put her head on his shoulders, and went to sleep a short time later. Her closeness and the motion of the carriage brought a contentment unlike anything he'd ever experienced.

He continued to peer out the window. Dusk fell subtly, then dusk fell away to a curtain of darkness.

They stopped for the night at the same inn they'd patronized on the northern leg of their journey. On their last visit, Nick had gone ahead and instructed his man to reserve the rooms for this date.

They were all exhausted from being cramped into their carriages for so many hours. Dinner was good and plentiful, and conversation was almost non-existent.

After dinner, they all said their good-nights and dispersed to their respective chambers.

Once Adam and Emma were in theirs, she turned around to face him, her expression solemn. She drew a breath. "I know I need practice, and I'm not very good at it, but I should love above everything for you to kiss me."

It was as if an avalanche of pent-up desires crashed down upon him. His whole body trembling, he drew her into his arms and kissed her ravenously. Her breath was as ragged as his when she stood on her tiptoes and wrapped her arms around him, giving every indication that she was enjoying this as much as he.

Letting out a deep breath, he released the pressure of his lips and nibbled tenderly at her mouth. Little whimpers of pleasure broke from her. She moved even closer. He felt as if he could explode from his want of this woman, *his wife*. Their mouths opened to one another—a prelude to that most intimate connection.

She did not kiss like a maiden. Even when his tongue slid into the warmth of her mouth, she did not recoil but welcomed it as greedily as a babe suckling its mother's breast.

"You need no instruction in kissing," he eventually murmured. "Your kisses are perfection." He sighed. He wanted her so much, but did she want him in the same way? He did not know how to ask. He did not want to offend her.

"I have enjoyed it very much." Her voice was as breathless as one who'd been . . . chopping wood!

He cupped his hand at her pretty little face. "I could never want any other woman for my wife." It wasn't a declaration of love, but it was close. He had never told a woman he loved her. He thought he was, indeed, falling in love with Emma, but he could never utter those words until he was certain.

Her torso pressed against him. *God help me*, he thought.

"Do you recall the vows we said before the priest at St. George's on our wedding day?" she whispered.

"What part?"

"The part about my body would be yours and yours would be mine."

She does want me!

Their eyes locked. He trembled so much and his breath was so labored he wasn't sure he could speak. "Does that mean you would not object if I were to . . . well, be your husband in every respect—just as the priest read?"

"I would not object."

He scooped her into his arms and carried her to the bed. *Their bed.*

$\mathcal{C}$hapter 21

He hadn't said it last night, but Emma knew Adam loved her. She now knew what it felt like to be cherished. Each caress, each kiss demonstrated his tender feelings toward her. She knew, too, what it felt like to be a wife. She knew what it was to be in love.

But she had not uttered those words to him, either. He must say it first. She had already made all the advances.

On this, the last day of their journey, they sat very close in the carriage, and neither she nor her husband seemed able to keep their hands off one another. She could not remove the smile from her face or the effervescence from her heart. She could shout her love of Adam from the spire of every church between here and London. What had she ever done to deserve such happiness?

Just as on the first day of their journey, she did not want this to come to an end. His house was awfully large, and as lovely as it was, she preferred the intimacy of this coach. It kept them so close, a sheet of paper could not have wedged between them.

"Are you not looking forward to being home?" Lady Sophia asked her.

Emma shook her head. "I have enjoyed every minute of this excursion—except for that one horrid night." Her gaze dropped to the red circles of oozing flesh at her wrists. They were healing. She wondered if Adam's tender kisses last night had aided in their visible recovery.

Even though that one night had been horrendous, all her physical and mental suffering was obliterated when Adam had drawn her into his arms. He had then given her to understand that losing her had made him realize how important she was to him.

Every second of her misery had been worth it for it solidified their love for one another.

"What could you possibly find to enjoy about being cooped up like this for days on end?" Lady Sophia asked.

"Many things. I acquired the experience of staying in an inn. Because it was a new experience for me, the anticipation was every bit as exciting as the actual stay."

The expression on William's face was one of incredulousness. "You mean you really enjoyed staying at an inn?"

Adam chuckled. "Something as lackluster as building supplies being drawn down the Strand inordinately excites my wife."

"It's because I'd spent all of my life in a village of less than one hundred people."

"Oh, dear," Lady Sophia exclaimed. "That certainly would limit the marriage pool."

Emma laughed. "Indeed. I had but one suitor, and the poor fellow was exceedingly dimwitted. He gave me a fright when he told me he'd proclaimed his love for me by carving into the Queen Elizabeth tree on the village common. I was relieved when I saw it for he misspelled my name."

"How could one misspell Emma?" Lady Sophia

asked, her brows lowered.

"I-M-A."

They all laughed.

"Pray," William asked, "what is the Queen Elizabeth tree?"

"The queen was supposed to have planted a tree in our village green on her progress north, but somehow she bypassed Upper Barrington—as is commonly done. Since they did not want to waste a good oak, one of my Lippincott ancestors went ahead and planted it, and it's been called the Elizabeth tree ever since."

"I would say," Lady Sophia said, "that it's most fortunate you left Nothing Barrington, came to London, and swept Adam off his feet."

It pleased Emma that they thought her marriage to Adam had begun as a love match. She hoped with all her heart it truly was one now. Emma tucked her arm into his. "I am very fortunate." She had started to say she was the most fortunate girl in all of England, but her husband would have been sure to chide her for speaking in hyperbole. But she most certainly *did* believe she was the most fortunate girl not only in England but in all the universe.

Because of the fair weather and the good roads, they reached London before dark. Before they left the carriage, Adam stealthily peered from his coach window to see if he could tell if someone was watching their house. He hadn't told them what he was doing, but Emma had come to know him very well—as he had come to know her.

This blending of minds, too, was part of being married. There was not a part of being married that she didn't enjoy.

"Any solo men lurking about, eyeing our

house?" she asked. It was the first time she had ever referred to the Curzon Street house as *our* house. Today was the first time she felt as if she truly was Adam's wife.

"Not that I can tell."

They said their farewells to William and Lady Sophia and climbed from the coach. "We're back at our home, my dear one."

He'd said it! Everything that had been his was now *ours*. She felt as if she walked on air as she strolled on her husband's arm to *their* front door.

* * *

The following morning, after they awakened in her bedchamber within each others' arms, Adam told her he had a very busy day.

"I must go to the bank, but before that, we shall go to Emmott's. It's been almost a week since we left those handwriting samples there. We ought to have an answer now."

"I know the answer already."

"I believe I do, too." Their eyes met. "You, by the way, are coming with me wherever I go." He climbed from the bed and began to get dressed.

She sat up in bed and watched him. "As much as I loathe James Ashburnham, I shall have to be grateful to him for keeping me by the person with whom I most want to share my life." *There!* She'd said nearly the same words to him that he'd said to her the first night of their lovemaking.

"You just haven't been around me long enough. You'll be glad when Ashburnham's brought to justice and you can be rid of me."

She pouted. "I almost wish he'd never be brought to justice."

A heated look on his face, he crossed the bedchamber, half dressed, and drew her into his arms, groaning. "Do you have any idea of the effect you have upon me?" He hungrily crushed his lips to hers.

Of this, too, she knew she would never tire.

* * *

As much as she had enjoyed their four days of carriage travel with William and Lady Sophia, Emma preferred being alone with her husband in their coach. This morning he pulled her onto his lap, and they partook of whispery, nibbly kisses between Mayfair and Holborn. They did not even mind when their carriage came to a complete stop for several minutes on the Strand, owing to the snarl of conveyances.

Neither irate hackney drivers, lads hawking hot chestnuts, nor the clatter of glass breaking could detract from her enjoyment of this short journey across London. The lashing of wind outside on this cool day only contributed to the sense of well-being she felt ensconced within the coach—with the man she loved.

As they neared Mr. Emmott's establishment, she saddened. It was so close to where her uncle's company was located. He must have ridden down this same street many times. She could not think of Uncle Simon and not feel cheated that she'd not gotten to meet him, angered that his life had been cut short.

Before they left the carriage, Adam buttoned her warm pelisse almost to her chin, and she placed her hands in the ermine muff. He, too, bundled up. "It's a blustery day. I'll not have you taking lung fever," he said.

She hadn't felt so cared for since she was a small girl.

In Mr. Emmott's office, they were once again

greeted in a most enthusiastic manner. "I am honored that you've graced my office, Mr. and Mrs. Birmingham. I was going to come see you today, sir," he said to Adam. "Please, have a seat. I wasn't sure if you'd be at the bank. Since you've gotten married, it seems you're spending less time at your establishment."

Adam nodded. "I pray my business is not suffering."

"Never that! It's the most successful bank in the kingdom. Something built on a great foundation will not crumble."

"We have actually been in Yorkshire this week to help my brother's electioneering."

"Yes, I read about Nicholas's candidacy. He will bring a great deal to Parliament."

"If he's elected," Adam said.

"The best man has to win, and this, most certainly, will be Nicholas."

"In our absence have you had any communication from Ashburnham about our challenge to Simon Hastings' will?"

Mr. Emmott shook his head. "But . . . I do have some hopefully welcome information to impart to you."

Adam's brows hiked. "About those handwriting samples?"

"Yes."

Emma sat up straighter, hardly able to contain her curiosity.

"All of your suspicions have been confirmed."

She and Adam exchanged happy glances.

"According to our expert, that address label does contain all the descenders that are found in the forged will. You will remember, they were incongruous with the rest of the handwriting in the will."

"And the letter purportedly from Faukes?" Adam asked.

"Forged. My expert confirmed your suspicions. Though it was a good forgery, again, the descenders were identical to those found in the address label. They did not match those that were verified to have been written by Mr. Faukes."

"Then all of this points to the fact that the will was forged by James Ashburnham," Adam said.

"Indeed it does."

"What's next?"

"Unless we can persuade him to drop his claim, I will try to bring him to trial."

Her eyes rounded. "Won't that take years?"

Emmott nodded. "Not only that, it will also eat up moneys the will would have provided."

"Nevertheless," Adam said, "I should like you to inform Ashburnham we have evidence against him and are prepared to litigate this matter."

Mr. Emmott nodded. "The letter will be drawn up and delivered to him today."

"I hate to bring this up," Adam said, "but we believe Mr. Ashburnham may have poisoned my wife's uncle. As much as I dislike the thought, perhaps we should have Hastings' body exhumed and tested."

"Proving her uncle was poisoned will not prove who administered the poison," Mr. Emmott said.

"That's true," Emma concurred. "I'm not sure we should go through with that at this time." She sighed. "I'm not sure I can bear it."

Adam took her hand and squeezed it.

* * *

Shortly after they arrived at the bank, where Adam introduced Emma to all his employees, Nick came. "I thought you'd be here," he said to Adam.

"And I knew you'd not be able to stay away from the Exchange. Is there anything you need to discuss with me?" Adam asked.

"No. I was early, so I thought I'd come and say hello." He eyed Emma. "If you need to catch up with your employees, I can stay a few minutes and chat with your charming wife."

Adam nodded. "Thanks. I do need to speak to Johnson." His gaze lingered on her for a moment before he walked away.

"Won't you sit by me on that sofa?" Nick asked.

Sometimes it seemed funny for her to hear Nick speak. Because he looked so much like Adam, she thought they would sound alike, but they didn't. Nick spoke much faster, and the tone of his voice was entirely different than her husband's.

"I was hoping to get you alone," he said.

Her brows lowered. "Is something wrong?"

He shrugged. "We are all, quite naturally, concerned about you and Adam. You can't possibly live a normal life as long as that threat lingers against you. I know Adam's nearly sick with worry."

"As much as I adore being with my husband every minute, I know the situation is unsustainable."

"William and I came up with what we thought was a solution, but Adam became enraged when we brought it up with him."

Her eyes narrowed. "Why?"

"Because he said it would endanger you."

"Go on."

"We believe that you could be a lure for this Ashburnham."

"I believe I already am."

"But with Adam constantly at your side, it's not likely Ashburnham will ever make a move."

"He must be brought to justice. What do you and William propose?"

"Adam needs to let you *appear* to walk about London alone. You wouldn't really be alone. The Birminghams have a creditable army of highly skilled men who would watch you at all times. They can be disguised as anything from a chimney sweep to a hackney driver."

"Let me ask you this. If Lady Fiona were in a situation comparable to mine, would you be able to allow her to walk about London alone? Would you entrust her safety to those Birmingham *soldiers*?"

He did not respond for a moment. "I don't know if I could."

"I assure you, Adam feels the same. He doesn't believe anyone could protect me as well as he can."

A slow smile hitched across Nick's face. "I knew the first night I met you that Adam was going to fall hard for you. It just happened faster than I thought."

"I was blessed neither with fortune nor great beauty, but for some unaccountable reason, I have been inordinately blessed to have won Adam's affection."

"Fiona and I have enjoyed watching you two fall in love."

He went to rise.

"Don't go. We need to discuss this plan of yours. I am most willing to use myself as bait. I completely trust Adam to see to my welfare. The difficulty is in finding some way in which he will be able to watch me without Ashburnham or his hired hand seeing him." She looked up at Nick. "For Adam will never consent to leaving my safety in the hands of others."

"I do understand. I couldn't let Fiona out of my sight under such circumstances."

"I'll talk to William. He'll know what to do. He spent years on the Continent eluding men intent on killing him."

As soon as he referred to William, he came strolling into the bank.

Nick told him Emma was willing to go ahead with their plan if they could think of a way that would allow Adam to observe her at all times without being detected.

"That's simple," William said. "We dress him like a woman. I've not faced the enemy yet who notices middle-aged or elderly women. Adam would have to decide if he wants a white wig or a . . . red one."

She couldn't imagine anything that would persuade Adam to dress as a woman.

"But you're considerably shorter than Adam," Nick protested. "Have you ever seen a woman over six feet tall?"

"Many times, though I will own, they're rare in our motherland." William thought for a moment. "He needs to be seated. That way his height won't be as pronounced. Sit a horse or drive a cart."

"That's contingent upon my husband approving."

"Hopefully, with your consent, he'll be more willing," Nick said.

Adam came to the reception area and greeted his brothers. "Have you not seen enough of me these past four days?"

"We had a matter of import to discuss with

your wife." Nick eyed the door to his brother's office. "Permit us to discuss this in private."

Once they were in the office, Emma spoke. "I think your brothers have a brilliant plan to catch Ashburnham."

Adam glared at William. "If it's the same as you brought up two nights ago, I'll have no part of it."

"But I will," she said. "I have no objection to using myself as bait—knowing my husband (as well as disguised Birmingham soldiers) will have me in his line of sight the whole time."

Still glaring, Adam asked William, "How do you propose to have me watching her without anyone seeing me?"

"You'll do as I've done many a time when I've found myself in a dangerous situation."

"What's that?" Adam asked.

"You'll dress as a woman."

Adam froze. Not a word was said.

They waited for his response.

Emma was certain he would never agree to it. First, he'd be too averse to leaving her alone. Second, his male pride wouldn't allow him to dress as a woman.

Finally, he spoke to William. "You're in charge of procuring wigs and dowdy clothing for a very tall woman."

Chapter 22

The following day William showed up at Curzon Street with a large sack.

"What the devil have you brought?" Adam asked.

"An assortment of women's wigs ranging in colour from white to red. You can't count on the plan succeeding the very first day. You'll want a different look each day so as not to attract notice." He removed them from his sack, one by one.

When he began to unload the used clothing, Adam groaned and looked at his wife. "I wouldn't do this for anyone else."

She moved to him and wrapped her arm about his waist. "I am most appreciative."

Even in broad daylight in front of his brother, her touch still had a profound effect upon him. He wondered if being with her would ever become mundane. He hoped to God she could always make him feel as she did today. He absently kissed the crown of her head.

"Go ahead," William said, "try on the clothing. At the bottom of the sack you'll find your bosom."

Emma began to giggle. "Forgive me, but the notion is just so comical."

He gave her a mock glare. "Do. Not. Laugh. At. Me."

"I'm sorry," she said.

He eyed his brother. "Do I have to have a bosom?"

William and Emma both nodded.

He heaved a sigh. "I will endeavor to don them, but don't expect me to model."

"As you like it," William said. "We just need to be sure they'll fit. You have to own, there aren't many women built like you."

In ten minutes Adam returned, a frown on his face. "I make a hideous woman."

"Just so long as you don't draw attention," William said. "We're striving for ordinary."

Adam rolled his eyes. "Just your average woman who's six feet, two inches tall."

"You'll be seated either on a horse or in a cart," Will said. "No one will know how tall you are."

"How many of our soldiers will also be watching my wife?" Adam asked.

"Half a dozen should do. Is that agreeable to you?"

"Yes. I just hate like the devil for them to see me dressed as a woman. Did you really resort to women's dress when you courted danger for king and crown?"

"Many times. A man will resort to anything to stay alive." William eyed Emma. "Or to protect the life of his wife."

"I think I'll look more natural if I'm riding with a man in a cart."

William nodded. "Then one of our soldiers will drive the cart. That will leave you free to race after Emma in the event of an abduction attempt."

"The cart can also be our arsenal," Adam said.

* * *

That afternoon, all by herself, she walked

through Hatchard's book shop on Piccadilly. Since Adam's library lacked a copy of *Lyrical Ballads*, she decided she would purchase it. Adam would probably want to have it bound in leather later. He went to a special book binder to ensure continuity on the shelves of his library.

Each man hovering in the shop aroused her suspicions. Was one of them the man Ashburnham had hired to grab her? But since she didn't see any men dressed coarsely as the man with the eye patch had been, she thought perhaps none of them had been hired by Ashburnham.

In the two times she'd seen James Ashburnham she'd been struck that he attempted to dress as a well-educated gentleman, but he fell far short. The ill fit of his clothing spoke to the fact he'd likely purchased them second-hand. Then when he spoke, it was obvious his voice was not that of a gentleman. Therefore, it would stand to reason the men Ashburnham hired would be of the same class as he.

She wondered, too, which of these men were Birmingham employees. Adam would have made certain one or two of their so-called soldiers would be with her every minute. She decided these soldiers would all be tall like her husband—which eliminated the slightly built young man of medium height who kept smiling at her. Her gaze discreetly fanned to each lone man. She would be hard pressed to pick one out as a Birmingham soldier. Every man in this book shop looked to be a gentleman.

But then, William would see to it that the disguises—even that of a well-dressed gentleman—were genuine.

It suddenly occurred to her the elderly woman

ambling from table to table in the book store was
no elderly woman. It was her husband! She would
not have recognized him. He had chosen the white
wig. "William's right," Adam had said earlier that
day. "No one takes notice of elderly women."

She and William both had promised they would
not laugh at him. Now that she was watching him
fully dressed as an elderly female, she admired
him. Laughter was the farthest thing from her
mind. Her husband would have made a fine actor.
But, then, Adam did everything well. Shakily, he
contorted himself to where his back bent as did
an elderly woman's. No one would ever think him
a handsome young man of six feet two.

As Emma strolled from table to table perusing
the books at Hatchard's, she found herself
wondering if Ashburnham even knew she had
returned to London. His ruthless employee *had*
been permanently silenced. Would Ashburnham
even learn of the death of the man he'd obviously
hired? No one in Wickley Glen had been able to
identify the dead man.

After leaving the book store, she strolled toward
Madame De Guerney's. She would inquire about
the progress on her presentation dress. Perhaps it
would be ready for a fitting.

The pavement seemed to be exceptionally
crowded today. While many of the lone men who
passed her were gentlemen, just as many were
not. A number of them dressed as Ashburnham
did in clothing that came from the second-hand
shops. Each one who passed caused her to
become queasy. *Was he the one?* she would ask
herself.

Any unease that petrified her would quickly be
forgotten when she remembered her husband was

close by, watching. How clever they had been to have him leave their home more than an hour before her. He'd gone to William's where he dressed, emerged a woman, and was assisted onto a fortified cart to sit next to one of the senior members of the Birmingham army. She'd been shocked to learn her husband's family needed so many highly qualified armed guards. It wasn't as if William was still dealing in gold bullion. Adam had explained that they still shipped large amounts of money throughout the Continent, as well as in the British Isles.

At Madame De Guerney's she was greeted enthusiastically by the owner. "Oh, Mrs. Birmingham, I am so happy you have come. Your beautiful gown is ready for a fitting. You have saved me a trip to Curzon Street."

How did the modiste know her home was on Curzon Street? Emma's heart sank. Had Maria lived there? Had Madame De Guerney brought Adam's mistress's gowns there? Thinking of Maria made Emma low. That explained why Adam had not told her he was in love with her. Hadn't he once told her that he would always love Maria?

Emma was confident that Adam loved her— first, like a stray pup, or a cherished relation— perhaps even as a lover.

But he was not *in love* with her as he'd so agonizingly been with his long-time mistress.

She tried on her gown, and when she peered in the looking glass, her eyes grew moist. *I am going to meet the queen.* A month earlier she would never have believed it. What a grand adventure she was having since she'd come to London.

The waist needed to be taken in a bit more, then Madame would have it delivered to her.

That's when Emma remembered that Madam's staff had delivered all her pretty dresses there shortly after her marriage.

Perhaps that odious Maria had not lived there. Emma sighed. Would she ever have the courage to ask Adam if Maria had ever lived at *their* house?

When she left the shop, she tried to surreptitiously determine if anyone gave the appearance of being interested in her, in following her. She didn't think anyone was. Many men as well as women crowded the pavement on either side of the busy street, and so many conveyances constantly swept past, seeing those on the other side of the street proved impossible.

The only way she could see those behind her was to stop and peer in the shop windows, which she frequently did. But no one seemed to be interested in her. What a pity all these Birmingham soldiers—and Adam, bless him—had gone to such lengths to nab Ashburnham and the evil men he associated with, and it was all for naught.

Ashburnham was most likely still waiting for the man with the eye patch to return from the north—with Emma. How long would it be before he even realized she'd gotten away, that his man had been killed?

She had watched carefully as her coach had pulled away from their house earlier that afternoon. Not a soul appeared to be following them.

How long would they have to keep trying to entrap Ashburnham? How long before he realized she had safely returned to London? How tedious this was going to be.

As she strolled along the pavement, she

casually moved her head toward the street and tried to catch a glimpse of the cart Adam was riding upon. She didn't see it. Of course, he would be following at a discreet distance. She could see him if she fully turned around, but she could not do that.

Even if all of this was for nothing.

On this stretch of the street, foot traffic was particularly thick. More than once she was bumped into. Being bumped into and having a strange man breathing down one's neck were two entirely different things. Now a man was practically affixing himself to her back. She walked faster. So did he. She was about to turn around and reprimand his rudeness when he spoke into her ear.

In a deep voice, he said, "Do not turn around, Mrs. Birmingham."

A chill coiled down her spine.

"If you value your husband's life you will do as I say. Turn left into the next lane. If you try to turn around, one of our men has been instructed to drive a stiletto into Mr. Birmingham's gut."

Trembling violently, she almost imperceptivity nodded. She did not want to make any move that would jeopardize Adam's life.

She quietly slid to her left at the next crossing. It was a very narrow alleyway which housed not a single place of business or residence.

A lone, banged-up, enclosed carriage blocked her progress. Its door flew open, and the man behind her picked her up and tossed her inside as if she were a sack of potatoes. He came and sat beside her.

"You're taking me to James Ashburnham," she said.

"I'm takin' ye to a place—a very private and remote place—where Mr. Ashburnham will be meeting with you."

Once he gets the information he wants, he's going to kill me.

Chapter 23

Why in the devil were there so many people moving about on the pavement today? Adam was having a bloody difficult time seeing his wife. It was rather like the crowds at Newmarket cheering on their horses—without the horses and without the cheering. Just a packed mass of humanity.

Emma's height—or lack of it—also contributed to his difficulty in seeing her. Several tall men walking behind her obscured her from his view. He regretted that he'd chosen to ride in the cart at a discreet distance behind her. "Can we not move up a bit more?" he asked the soldier driving the cart.

"If you'd like." The driver flicked the ribbons, and they gained several feet on the pedestrians to their right.

When her ermine bonnet came into view, he sighed with relief, but he didn't like the way the man behind her was pressing so closely against her. "Stay at this pace. I want to keep her in our view."

She began to move to her right. She likely wanted to get away from the rude man behind her.

Adam tensed. The damned man was also moving to the right!

She slipped into an alley.

That man followed her.

Fear knotted inside him. What the hell was she doing? "Stop!"

Adam leapt from the cart. He was knocked to the ground by a horse coming up on their right. "Watch where yer going! You could be killed," the horseman shouted.

Adam got up and tried to race toward the pavement, toward that alley. His blasted knee hurt like the devil. Limping, he pushed through the pedestrians and rounded the corner onto the alley.

His heart stopped.

A dilapidated coach sped down the alley and rounded the corner to the next street.

He started after it, running as fast as he could on the injured knee. He didn't care about the pain. All that mattered was getting her.

One of his own soldiers flew past him. When he reached the point where the carriage had turned, he stopped. Adam caught up with him.

There was no sign of the coach.

He wife had been abducted. Ashburnham would kill her this time.

Adam had to save her.

* * *

Just when Emma's wrists were starting to heal, the rough rope which bound her hands in front of her cut into the sore flesh. And once again, a thick cloth covered her mouth. She couldn't even ask where she was being taken.

An abduction in broad daylight meant Ashburnham was desperate. He was going to kill her.

I've brought this upon myself. She had offered to be bait. How could a simple clerk have outwitted all those Birmingham soldiers as well as her husband? She'd put too much faith in Adam's abilities. Now she suffered the consequence of her naiveté.

She had imbued her husband with every admirable trait a man could possess. Not only that, she was convinced he was *the* best in the world at each. Nothing could possibly happen to her when one as perfect as Adam was watching her.

Wherever they were taking her, it wasn't close to Piccadilly. They rode along for nearly an hour. Through a frayed hole in the curtains at the carriage window she could glimpse the narrow streets they sped along, glimpse the even narrower buildings in various stages of decay. This was a section of London she'd not yet seen.

They must be drawing nearer to the Thames because the foghorns sounded closer. The rickety houses gave way to huge warehouses. It was to one of these they took her.

The coach came to a stop. The brute next to her threw open the door, disembarked, and yanked her out. She surveyed her surroundings. Not a soul could be seen. Across the lane was an abandoned building, its windows either missing or broken, part of its roof caved in. The building in front of them also appeared to be abandoned.

Even if her mouth had not been bound, she couldn't have called for help. There was no one to hear her in so isolated a place.

It was just her, her captor, and the man who'd driven the carriage. Both men were fairly youthful, and both looked vaguely familiar. It took her a moment to realize the two bore a strong resemblance to James Ashburnham. They must be his brothers. Kinship produced loyalty. She had no hope of buying them off. Even if she could speak.

A brother got on each side of her, grabbing her upper arms, as they forced her into the building to their front. On the ground floor, crates from the Ceylon Tea Company were stacked—confirmation that James Ashburnham was responsible for her abduction. Would he also be her murderer?

They went up a flight of stairs, careful to avoid boards where the old wood had rotted away.

"Is my husband being kept here?"

Her captor laughed. "We don't have yer husband. 'Twas a ploy to kidnap you."

Did that mean there was hope that Adam could still find her?

At the top of the stairs. she was shoved into a small room. A mouse scurried across the sagging floor and squeezed beneath the floorboards. The men slammed the door behind her. A lock bolted.

When she heard their steps descending the stairs, she was relieved that she was to be left alone.

For a while.

She went to the musty chamber's only window. Though it was streaked with decades of dust and dirt, she could peer at the barges and ships that floated down the river below. At one time, this warehouse must have been used for shipping.

Was there a way to escape? She turned back and surveyed the ten-foot-square room. Its dusty wooden floors showed signs of neglect and age. Nothing else was in the chamber except a handful of nails. She went to the door and tried the lock. Her hands might be tied, but they weren't useless. No matter how much she attempted to jiggle the door, the lock held. Why was it the only thing in the building that was solid was that blasted lock? There was no way anyone would ever find her here, no way she could ever extricate herself.

* * *

Adam had never felt so helpless. Or hopeless. He had failed Emma.

"No way we can we catch that coach," the soldier, Helmsworth, said to him.

"I know." He froze there for several moments, numb with fear and stupefied by his own powerlessness.

All he knew to do was to go for Ashburnham on the off chance it would lead to Emma.

"Get my brother William and tell him I've gone to the Ceylon Tea Company in Southwark. I'll send the other soldiers there."

* * *

He'd not trust that nag-driven cart to speed him through the Capital. They drove it to Nick's place at the other end of Piccadilly. Because his brother's town home was the largest in London, it housed a sizeable stable. Adam swapped his nag and cart for one of Nick's fleet-footed beasts, as did the pair of soldiers who had not mounted a horse. While his mount was being saddled, he raced into his brother's house, tossing off his woman's wig and shawl as he hastened to Nick's bedchamber and quickly threw on—with Nick's valet's help—*men's* breeches, boots and shirt. He didn't take time to tie a cravat. They all took off at a manic pace along the city's busy streets.

His confidence that his horse could move far more quickly than any carriage paid off. He pulled up in front of the tea company in a matter of minutes. The same journey in a coach at this time of day would have taken nearly an hour.

He raced upstairs and came to a halt in front of Ashburnham's empty desk. Then he remembered that the clerk had moved into Simon Hastings' old office. Its door was open, but there was no sign of Ashburnham. Hoping against hope, Adam sped to Fauke's office and threw open the door. "Where's Ashburnham?"

"He just received word that he was needed elsewhere and left. I didn't ask where. I assumed there was trouble with one of our customers."

Adam cursed. "Where does he live?"

Faukes shrugged. "All I know is that he lives in Southwark."

"There must be something that has the man's address!"

"You might ask the fellows in shipping down below. Perhaps one of them knows."

Downstairs, Adam questioned each man. One by one, they shook their heads. When he reached the final worker, a burly young man who could not yet have reached twenty, that man nodded. "I've never been to Mr. Ashburnham's house, but I seen him walk there many times. It's on me own way home from work."

"Come. Show me."

To the knot of soldiers gathered outside the tea company, Adam said, "Follow us!"

William came pounding up on a stallion, and as they rode through Southwark, Adam tired to explain—in short bursts—what had happened.

The street where Ashburnham lived was about a mile from the tea company. The Birmingham brothers dismounted and gave orders that the building be surrounded.

The extremely narrow house was of the style

built more than a hundred years earlier. Not unexpectedly, the street was very quiet, given that people who lived in so modest a neighborhood had to work for a living.

Adam dispensed with knocking on the door. He tried the handle. It was locked. He then tried to smash himself into the door. It held.

William stepped over to the house's only ground-floor window and butted the hilt of his knife into it. It shattered.

William cleared away the broken glass to open it, climbed through the opening, and let his brother in the front door. The two men, swords drawn, went from room to room, searching for Ashburnham. There were two shabby rooms down, two room up. And no Ashburnham.

The only place he could have hidden was under the lone bed, but nothing was there.

How would they ever find Emma in a city as vast as London?

Chapter 24

Footsteps mounted the stairs. One person's. A man. Fear choked her. It must be Ashburnham. How much time did she have left before he killed her?

Her efforts to free herself of the tightly knotted rope around her wrists had failed. Everything had failed.

And now she would die.

A key went into the lock, the handle twisted, and the door opened. Ashburnham stood framed in the doorway. He was not a large man, not large at all, but no one had ever looked so menacing. A sneer dragged on his mouth, and he eyed her with palpable hatred. "I should have killed you that first week."

She straightened her spine. She did not want to appear a defenseless female, though that was exactly what she was. "You are a fool if you think my husband would not avenge my death. Do you have any idea how powerful he is?"

He laughed a mirthless laugh. "If I can nab you, I can trick him. Nobody gives me credit for being the genius I am. I can slay him—and get away with it. You think he's powerful. It's I who's the powerful one. No one can defeat James Ashburnham."

"You're already defeated. We have proof that

you forged my uncle's will. We have proof you forged the note from Mr. Faukes. We will soon have proof that my uncle was poisoned. It does not take a genius to follow the crimes to the one person who benefits from them."

"With you and your husband dead, there will be no one to challenge the will. You're Simon Hastings' last surviving relation."

"My husband's solicitor knows everything, and his loyalty to the Birmingham family ensures that he will see you hang."

Ashburnham shrugged. "A convenient *accident* will silence him."

"You're delusional."

He came closer. "You've told me everything I needed to know. Your husband and Emmott will also have to be silenced." He started walking toward her, his hands balled into fists.

"There are others!"

He stopped. "Who?"

"I shan't tell you."

He moved to her and closed his sweaty hands around her neck.

* * *

"Back to the tea company!" Adam ordered. Faukes might know of a place where Ashburnham would be keeping Emma. Since he'd not yet come into a penny of Hastings' money, it wasn't likely Ashburnham would have the funds for another place. He had to be hard pressed for cash, especially given that he was hiring brutes to capture a defenseless female.

They all rode as if a wildfire leapt at their heels, and they reached Faukes' business in less than two minutes.

He burst into Faukes' office. "Ashburnham's got

my wife. We've got to find her before she ends up like her uncle!"

William stepped forward and addressed Faukes. "Is there any building you know of, a place where he might have taken her? A place in an unpopulated area?"

His brows lowered, Faukes shook his head solemnly.

Adam winced. God in heaven, what was he to do? "We've got to send our men to every corner of the city. We've got to find her." He knew that looking for a needle in a haystack would have been far easier.

A sickness in his gut, he began to leave Faukes' office. His poor little Emma. How he wished he could die with her so she wouldn't have to be alone.

He'd never see her again. It sickened him even more to realize he had never told her he loved her. God, but he loved her! She was the best thing that ever happened to him.

"Wait!" Faukes said.

Adam turned back and froze with profound hope.

"We used to have an auxiliary warehouse near the docks, but we abandoned it because the roof was bad, and the quay had become useless."

"Where?" Adam demanded.

"I'll show you."

$\mathcal{C}$hapter 25

She could not scream. She could not slap him. But she could move. She wasn't about to be trapped in a corner.

With her bound hands, she lifted her skirts as he moved toward her, and with every ounce of strength in her body, she jammed her knee into his groin.

He screamed like a woman and fell to the floor.

Thank God he'd left the door open! She raced to it. Just as she reached the doorway, his hand caught her dress and yanked.

She fell just feet away from where he'd landed. She tried to propel herself toward the open doorway, but he wouldn't let go of her dress. A string of vile curses flowed from his vile mouth. Fortunately, his obvious pain prevented him from moving quickly.

Whenever his pain abated, she knew he would regain his strength and strangle the life from her. She kicked at him. He grabbed her foot and cursed some more. She tried to kick him with her other foot but could not quite reach him. How could she get away from his deathly grasp? She was no match for him in strength.

Minutes passed. His curses trailed off as his pain subsided. Her heart drummed. *He's going to kill me now.*

Still digging his fingers into her foot, he sat up. His green eyes bore into hers as he moved toward her. He then did a most peculiar thing. He straddled her as if she were a horse.

His hands closed around her throat. "You will tell me who else knows." His grip tightened.

She felt as if her windpipe collapsed. "I'll not tell you," she croaked.

He squeezed harder. "I think you will."

She felt as if she could not breathe. Panic set in. She shook her head rapidly.

"Tell me who else knows. Does your husband's brother know? That fellow who rules the Exchange?"

Nick. She had nothing to lose. He would kill her if she did not tell him, and he'd kill her if she did. She probably couldn't answer because her throat was so restricted, but she wasn't about to try.

Her only consolation in death was the knowledge that the Birminghams would hunt him down like a mangy dog.

She flashed a defiant gaze at him.

"Why, you . . . " His hands choked her harder.

Now she really could not breath. Involuntarily, her eyes closed, and she felt as if she were falling into a dark well.

From far off she heard Adam's voice. "Get your foul hands off my wife!"

* * *

Adam raced toward Ashburnham and leveled a kick right in the man's face. The clerk went sailing backward, curse words spouting.

"I'll take care of him," William yelled. "See to Emma."

Her eyes closed, she looked as if she were dead. The imprint of Ashburnham's fingers whitened against the blue of her neck. Blinding rage filled Adam. *I'll kill him.*

Tears spilling from his eyes, he lifted her into his arms and cradled her, weeping. "Please don't die." He kissed her hair, kissed her cheeks, and finally drew a gasping breath and pressed his lips to her blue mouth.

They were warm. She wasn't dead! "My God, Emma, I can't lose you. I love you!" His breath hitched. "I love you with all my aching heart."

Her lids fluttered. She mumbled, "I was *dying* to hear those words."

He held her tighter. And wept.

$\mathcal{E}$ pilogue

Two weeks later . . .

The bloody circles around her wrists no longer bled. The blue circle around her neck was fading. James Ashburnham was in Newgate Prison charged with murder. But still her husband had not returned to his bank. He refused to leave her side.

Not that she minded. She never tired of being with him, never tired of being cherished by this man she loved more than life.

This was the first day he had allowed her out of their house since the day James Ashburnham had nearly killed her. Adam's ministrations on her behalf were growing tedious. As much as she basked in his love and as much as she admired their beautiful house, she needed to get away, and so did he.

They sat close in the carriage, each of them touching and feeling and kissing the other. She would never tire of these actions.

As the coach rattled over the busy streets of the Capital, she reflected on that horrid day James Ashburnham tried to kill her. She was quite sure she was almost dead when she heard Adam declare his love for her. From the edge of oblivion, she clawed back. Because of Adam. Because of his love for her.

"I have a confession," she said.

He pulled her closer. "And what might that be?"

She drew a deep breath. "Since the day I married you, I've been in love with you."

He smiled. "That's hardly a confession. A confession's a revelation about something wicked." Drawing her even closer, he growled, "Unless you're admitting you've always had wicked thoughts about me."

She playfully swatted at him. "I didn't know about wickedness until you introduced me to it."

He kissed her hungrily and splayed his hand over her breast. "In this way?"

Her breath was coming fast. "You're very wicked."

"I have a confession, too."

She raised her brows.

"Nick told me I had never married because I'd not met The One." He paused. Swallowed. "You are The One."

Her eyes moist, the former Miss Emma Hastings was speechless.

He drew her into his arms. "Where is it you're taking us today, love?"

"I'm not telling you until we get there."

"Why the secrecy?"

"It's not really secret. It's just that I was afraid you wouldn't want to come. You'd find it too somber after all we've been through."

Their carriage came to a stop. She peered from the coach window and realized they'd arrived at their destination.

The coachman let down the step and opened the door. Adam looked around. "You've brought me to a bloody cemetery?"

She nodded playfully as he assisted her from

the coach. "It's where Uncle Simon is buried."

He bowed his head and adopted a solemn countenance.

"You mustn't be mournful," she said. "I'm very sorry for his death and very sorry that I never met him, but I owe so much to him."

It was then that the coachman handed her the flowers she had pre-selected to place on her uncle's grave. She and Adam walked along the old cemetery until they found the granite marker. She grew solemn as she read her uncle's name and the dates of his birth and death. Leaning over the grave, she placed the wreath against the headstone.

"I know it's silly," she said, "but I wanted to tell Uncle Simon that I've decided to use the money he left to me to establish an orphanage in London. I was a fortunate orphan to have had Aunt Harriett and Uncle Simon. Most others, especially here in London, aren't as lucky. Because of Uncle Simon, orphans for decades to come will have a home and opportunities to succeed in life."

Adam nodded his agreement.

"And, Uncle Simon," she said, looking at his headstone, "I want you to know that because of your death, I've had the great good fortune to unite myself with the most wonderful man in the world. It would never have happened had you not died." She recalled the rainy night of her arrival in London, the night she met her husband. What could have been disastrous for her turned into an unrivaled advantage.

Adam moved directly behind her and pulled her against him, encircling her in his arms. "Permit me to address your uncle."

Happiness flashing in her eyes, she nodded.

"I will cherish your niece until the stars cease to shine, until the end of time."

She turned around to face him, tears glistening in her eyes. "I think Uncle Simon would approve."

He drew her into his arms for a tender kiss.

The End

Author's Biography

A former journalist and English teacher, Cheryl Bolen sold her first book to Harlequin Historical in 1997. That book, *A Duke Deceived*, was a finalist for the Holt Medallion for Best First Book, and it netted her the title Notable New Author. Since then she has published more than 20 books with Kensington/Zebra, Love Inspired Historical and was Montlake launch author for Kindle Serials. As an independent author, she has broken into the top 5 on the *New York Times* and top 20 on the *USA Today* best-seller lists.

Her 2005 book *One Golden Ring* won the Holt Medallion for Best Historical, and her 2011 gothic historical *My Lord Wicked* was awarded Best Historical in the International Digital Awards, the same year one of her Christmas novellas was chosen as Best Historical Novella by Hearts Through History. Her books have been finalists for other awards, including the Daphne du Maurier, and have been translated into eight languages.

She invites readers to www.CherylBolen.com, or her blog, www.cherylsregencyramblings.wordpress.co or Facebook at https://www.facebook.com/pages/Cheryl-Bolen-Books/146842652076424.